Foreword

The great honor of my life is to have served in the company of heroes. In captivity in Vietnam, we fought every day to keep our honor intact, our minds sharp, and bodies functional. John Borling, a POW for over six and a half years, won this fight for himself and contributed greatly to the morale and survival of the rest of us with his poems and incredible talent for storytelling.

Taps on the Walls: Poems from the Hanoi Hilton reveals John's incredible creative and mental effort. Surviving alone or in semi-isolation, John first used his poetry as a weapon to "stay sharp." Using the forbidden tap code, his poems were tapped through the walls from one POW to another to boost morale and, as a legacy for his wife Myrna in case he didn't make it home. He did survive and went on to become a General Officer in the Air Force.

I met John after the Son Tay raid in November 1970. While that raid failed to liberate any prisoners, it forced the consolidation of POWs into larger groups at the Hanoi Hilton—a remarkable blessing. If you have never been deprived of liberty in solitude, you cannot know the ineffable joy you experience in the open company of other human beings, free to talk and joke without fear. The strength we acquired through fraternity with our fellow soldiers was immeasurable.

This environment brought forth the talents of men like John, whose prowess as a teller of tales and as a poet was already well-known. In the larger group, he would entertain us with stories from a movie or a book—making them live in our imaginations with all the reality of a movie screen or a printed page. His personal collection of poetry, mentally composed and memorized over the course of his imprisonment, was another valuable source of mental stimulation and discussion.

It is most fitting that on this 40th year anniversary of our release from prison in Vietnam that you can know and appreciate John's remarkable work as we did during our darkest days in the Hanoi Hilton. Keeping a sense of humor while in prison was indispensible to our survival. John's words express that humor and more, as there are some stories of the soul that extend far beyond prison walls. Enjoy.

Senator John McCain
POW, North Vietnam, 1967-1973

Introduction

This is a story about the power of the unwritten word. It is a redemptive story—how poetry helped save me during six and a half years as a POW in North Vietnamese prison camps.

Ubon Air Base, Thailand: Flying combat for six months. On 1 June 1966, my life changed forever.

My 97th fighter mission was a volunteer-only night sortie deep into the heart of heavily defended North Vietnam. Three more flights north after this one and I'd be finished with my hundred-mission tour. With orders in hand to a fighter base in England, there was good duty ahead. Actually, pretty far ahead, because I had volunteered to fly another hundred missions before leaving the combat zone.

So, on that bright, moonlit June night, it was low and fast over the mountains northeast of Hanoi in an F-4 Phantom. Reaching the target area, heavy ground fire ripped into the jet. Out of control. No controls. Upside down. The jet was dead. I had to get out. Eject. Ejected and hit the ground; it was that close.

I hit on a long, steep, furrowed hill and went bouncing downhill like some kind of crazy jumping bean and ended up in a beat-up heap at the bottom. That hill probably saved my life. I was alive, but with disabling pain in my back, ribs, and ankles. There was blood everywhere. I couldn't walk. I was broken. The locals were all around me, shooting into the bushes and jungle to flush me out. I had to get away. I crawled into a log and passed out.

When I came to, they were gone. I heard truck traffic maybe fifty yards away on Highway One, which led northeast to China. There was no rescue possible. I was in too deep. I had to get out on my own. I had to break the no-contact-with-the-enemy rule. I would hijack a truck and make them drive me to the coast. Then I'd commandeer a boat and head south. It seemed like a good plan at the time. It was the only plan that made sense. Surrender was not a plan.

It took a long time crawling, but finally, beggarlike, clutching my service revolver, I huddled on the side of the road. A truck came at me. I yelled and waved my gun. Nothing; it rolled on by.

Shit. I needed to be in the road. Had to make 'em stop or run over me. A branch became a crutch, and I struggled out to the middle of the rutted track. A couple minutes later, another truck. I waved my gun and stared down the driver. That did it. Success. I had jacked a truck.

Unfortunately, it was a truck full of North Vietnamese regular troops. Despite my shouted orders to surrender, they didn't. I ended up tied up, stripped naked, and lying in the road.

That's how it began. Twenty-four hours later, I was dragged into the infamous Hoa Lo prison (aka the Hanoi Hilton). I would be a POW for more than six years and eight months. My wife would not know if I was alive for years. Somehow, she "felt me" and carried on while all others doubted. My nine-month-old daughter would grow and dream of a father walking her to school one day.

I would have the same dream. She would be seven and a half before our dreams came true.

But happy endings would come hard, with hate, horror and humor, honor and shame coming first. Horses of hope (or hopelessness) galloped for years with no finish line in sight. God was very close or very distant. Freedom and flying were unreachable stars.

For many years, my fellow pilots and I were held alone or in semi-isolation. The enemy wanted us weak, despondent, and totally cut off. Our challenge was to keep the faith, carry on, and stay true to one another. For that, we had to communicate.

Communication among prisoners in different cells was forbidden and severely punished. The enemy called us war criminals and threatened trial and execution. In reality, they were too cruel to kill us and preferred prolonged privation, pain, and humiliation. We struggled with multiple illnesses, untreated wounds, toothaches, horrific heat and surprising cold, lack of food and water, a bucket (often overflowing) for a toilet, and a board with a straw mat for a bed. Thank God for a mosquito net, which they took away in the isolated punishment cells. The hardest struggle was filling the endless, empty days.

So, we tapped on the walls. The tap code became our lifeline, our means of passing along information and words of encouragement to one another. Besides our knuckles, we used anything that carried sound to tap the code. Rhythmically sweeping a stiff bamboo broom, a fellow POW assigned to clean an area could send messages.

Coughs worked. At times the place sounded like a tuberculosis ward. Mostly, we tapped on the walls.

We tapped names so others would know and remember who was alive. We tapped messages of hope and family. We tapped jokes. We tapped interrogator questions and our common policy answers to maintain solidarity. We tapped about hurt and sickness. We tapped to teach and learn languages. We tapped prayers, lots of prayers. We tapped as if our lives depended on tapping—because they did.

When caught communicating or breaking other insane "war criminal rules," we were hurt and hurt badly, suffering severe physical and psychological pain. Despite the punishment, we persisted. We stayed organized and resisted as best we could. Some bent, some broke, and some died, but, with rare exception, we stayed true to one another. The years passed, and we kept tapping on the walls.

I also tapped poems.

Jail me, hurt me, hate me, but I had my mind and spirit as weapons. No books, no writing materials, nothing—just the mind. Find a way. Each man had to find his own way to use time.

One of the ways for me was to mentally create poetry. Create and memorize lots of poetry as a way to fight back. The U.S. Air Force Academy's heavy science curriculum also included a good dose of the liberal arts. I had always loved English and literature and acquired a modest appreciation of poetic structure and pattern. Anyway, every man in love is inspired to verse (or should be). Pre-shoot-down excursions of the heart to Myrna now had new value as to form and rhyme. Fragments and, at times, whole poems were tapped through the walls. Kipling ("If" and "The Ballad of East and West"), Service ("The Cremation of Sam McGee" and "The Shooting of Dan McGrew"), Shakespeare (fragments of any kind), and Henley's "Invictus." Mental hunger was easily the most ravenous. Poetry was my meat and potatoes.

In Hanoi, the poetic way was marred, even blocked, by the need to open an armored heart and mind to limitless expression. That expression, that exposure to real or even imagined life, really hurt. Notwithstanding the mental hurt, the process of creating and memorizing my "treasures of the mind" proved a joyful and needed task. Tapping on the walls, fellow POWs memorized my poems to provide a legacy for Myrna in case I didn't survive and as a mental exercise of their own.

The verse and prose in this volume are not principally about pain or pity, but more about the essence of the human condition. That essence was and is the ability to create. Creating provided a pathway to survival and salvation. The process of creating made enemy time an ally, and an uncertain race could be run.

It's possible to divide the prisoner-of-war experience into three approximate periods. The early years up to late 1969 and early 1970, were brutal, with little if any respite. Alone or in semi-isolation, we still insisted on a chain of command and adherence to the military code of conduct.

Though separated physically, we helped one another resist enemy pressures to break us down. "Do your best" (translation: "Make them really hurt you before you give them anything"), then "Bend, don't break" ("Keep resisting"). Don't self-torture. Keep communicating.

Locked in squalid cells, we tried to preserve dignity through the many months and years. We held on to the belief that our country would not let us down. We would go home. We would love again. We would fly again. We tried to stay sane.

After Ho Chi Minh's death and the Son Tay raid in 1970, conditions improved gradually, leading to a third period approximating a more normalized POW experience shortly before our release in 1973. Gross exceptions abound to this general observation, and cruelty to some or many was still a reality even up to the end in 1973. Suffice to say, the Geneva Conventions and protocols were never respected. Not even close.

My poems stretch across those time lines and reflect the realities of treatment and personal physical and mental health, or lack of same. There is an intended balance, however, between pleasure and pathos, humor and horror, and multiple themes cutting across the years.

Taps on the Walls is divided into four sections. You will read of a passion for the sky and a great missing of the freedom that flying provides in "Strapping on a Tailpipe." The dark, hard days are in "POW and Other 'Dark and Bitter Stuff' " and "The Holidays and Hollow Days," when the awful loneliness and extended isolation were fought with the need to remember, celebrate, and be grateful. "SEA Story" in Section IV is an epic poem that took many years to write and, if read carefully, offers commentary on just about everything. The glossary will help those unfamiliar with military, aviation, and historical terms.

During the last year of the war, on the whole, conditions improved. This varied from camp to camp. Was the end in sight? We experienced more group living and time outside. We received some books, some heavily pilfered packages from home, and finally a few letters—six-line letters. The diet improved, and we gained weight.

Peace came in January 1973 after a Christmas bombing campaign by the United States that hit, among other high-value assets, military targets in downtown Hanoi (a campaign that should have been launched in early 1966). It was considered, I know. As a junior officer on a planning team in Saigon, I helped formulate Operation Reprisal, a high-intensity air campaign designed to break enemy will and capability and end the war. The plan was rejected in Washington. Seven years later, we had more than 58,000 American troops killed, hundreds of thousands wounded, plus the captured, the missing, and the still missing. When will we ever learn?

When you are in it, war is very personal. For me, thousands of days and thousands of words later, my first and personal war was over.

12 February 1973 was my day of release. We were going home with honor. After being flown to Clark Air Base in the Philippines, we were hospitalized, and the

debugging and the deworming and the de-thising and de-thating started. The doctors were amazed by our resiliency and reliance on one another. They expected freaks but instead got a bunch of fighter pilots eager to get back to some serious living.

I called Myrna in Illinois. It was a great call, just like I'd gone out for a pack of cigarettes and was home again. We agreed that I would stay in the Air Force and go back to flying fighters. If I was any good, we would stay in and compete for a "normal" career. If not, I'd get out. She told me, as always, that she was flying with me. As we relaunched our marriage in the following months, she was more often the leader and I was on the wing.

After we talked, still in a bathrobe, I snuck out to the Base Exchange to get a tape recorder so I could start downloading the poems. The manager came back with a shoebox-looking thing and I protested, "Not a radio, a tape recorder—you know, with reels and stuff." He laughed and gave a cassette recorder to the now future-shocked ex-POW.

My poems came home with me. Intensely private, they stayed with me. Now, these many years later, on the fortieth anniversary of release, we stand ready for scrutiny.

They remain pieces of my soul. I hope they become pieces of yours.

The Tap Code

The tap code was our primary means of communication. Captain (now retired Colonel) Carlyle Smith "Smitty" Harris, a 1965 shoot down, was credited with importing and passing on the code.

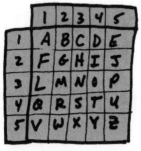

The easy-to-learn code uses a 5 x 5 square numbered from 1 to 5 horizontally along the top and then again vertically down the left side, with the letters of the alphabet running in order across each row of boxes.

Each letter is tapped with two numbers. The first tap signifies which horizontal row is being used, and the second signifies which vertical column for each letter. By example, to send the letter "O," tap three times, quick pause, then tap four times on the cell wall. Roger, or "Got it," was two taps (normally after every word). "Don't understand" or "Repeat" was a rapid series of taps. "Call up" was "shave and a haircut." The letter "C" is used for "K," or tapped as 2,6. For example "pilot" is tapped 3,5 2,4 3,1 3,4 4,4.

* * * *

Nightly sign-off was "GBU" 2,2 1,2 4,5: God Bless You.

And I hope that for you.

433rd Tactical Fighter Squadron Mates
Bar, Ubon Air Base, Thailand,
1966

Section I

Strapping on a Tailpipe

Question: *"What's it feel like—flying fighters?"*

Answer: *"It's the most fun you can have with your clothes on."*

Question: *"Mommy, when I grow up, can I be an Air Force pilot?"*

Answer: *"Sorry, dear, you can't do both."*

"The sky is the only perfect place."
—**Richard Bach**

"Let's go there now a little while."
—**John Borling**
Call Sign: "Viking"

The Derelict

The west was a patchwork of color flung over a racing sky,
The wind was a lover's whisper that needed no reply,
The strip was of weed-torn concrete, scarring the desert floor,
And a derelict came flying,
Flying, flying,
A derelict came flying,
Long final to zero four.

Over the sentry saguaro and ancient access road,
Its gear and flaps full down and locked,
Ball turret position stowed.
Across the wasted overrun and into a practiced flare,
Then dust was blown at the bleached end,
A puff of smoke at the bleached end,
And tail wheel touched tarmac there.

A fuselage of mottled brown, the dirty greens and black,
Along the crusted taxiway,
Chin turret guns hung slack.
Its wings were streaked to the trailing edge,
Black square, white D on the tail,
And it came, the outboards throbbing,
The cyclones, outboard, throbbing,
It came like a lost child, sobbing,
Searching to no avail.

Line's edge and the question: Rest or roam?
It paused and seemed to stare,
An apron expanse of loneliness,
The ramp lay withered and bare.
Grey clapboard beyond and rusting tin
Vacantly weather away.
The tower door on a broken hinge,
Marks time with an aimless sway.
A throttle burst brings no answer,
Nor trooping the line's empty glare,
A review of past disappointments and departures of despair.

No use to wish or to linger,
No good to wonder why.
The Fort will return to the runway,
Unable to live or die.
Takeoff roll and a farewell drone,
Unheard in the desert air,
Outbound in search of home again,
Trying to go home again,
And all who follow it home again,
Will never find it there.

First-Light Flight

Pale golden talons stir the eastern sky;
Another fledgling day departs the hills.
It takes the air as thermaled falcons fly,
Cascading light as carefree first-flight thrills.
And who attends this noble soaring birth,
From mountain crag to gentle rolling plain,
May marvel from their vantage point on earth,
Yet miss so much, not of the sky's domain.
But I'm not of the earth. At altitude,
I greet the infant day with engine song,
My contrails etched on endless morning blued,
And rare abandon urging me along.
It's here, unfettered brother men enthrall
To first-light flight, the one judged best of all.

The Boneyard

Alone, I walked a desert path
Beneath a sky of red.
Along a fence that split the world,
Perchance, a heart instead.

I viewed the metal might of man
In motionless parade,
And through the mesh reviewing stand,
Saw legends that were made.

They'd faced the flak and fearsome skies
Of Schweinfurt and Rabaul,
Then air-dropped candy to Berlin,
And stalked the Yalu hall.

See manifested from within,
Their tarnished hulks a string
Of beer and bombs, the coal and kids,
So freedom's bell could ring.

Young ones, parts newly stripped away,
Stand numb in disbelief,
And wonder how they came to be
Upon this dreaded fief.

Veterans in resignation wait,
Struts sunk into the sand.
And though gloss gone and fabric ripped,
Still strangers to the land.

All bear the cross called lack of need,
Old age or obsolete.
They're scourged beneath the sky they love,
Along a desert street.

A pilot's judgment can't be heard,
Above the roaring din.
The shouts that cry out crucify,
And keep the dollars thin.

So they're confined, judged guilty of
Duty dereliction.
All slumped in rigid sacrifice,
Hoping resurrection.

Don't think about the giant press
That makes proud metal cry.
Recall the adage, timeworn too,
"Always the other guy."

Yes, this is an aircraft boneyard,
A desert dying bed.
Here hope was strong, but hope is gone,
Among the sleeping dead.

Some would say aircraft cannot feel,
Hence cannot know their lot.
Such is the theme for all things old,
Not needed: Let 'em rot.

Unknowing superior man,
I scorned along with thee,
Till one night, wakened from deep sleep,
I heard them calling me.

Go back to sleep, I told myself,
And not another thought.
Still, lying there, I could not find
The rest and peace I sought.

Feeling foolish, I walked the fence
That cold dark desert night,
Till asked a shadow at my side,
"Hey buddy, got a light?"

The shiver started at my heart,
And ran from neck to toe.
That tingling fear of things unknown,
Nowhere for me to go.

He smiled and cocked his ancient cap,
With fifty-mission crush,
Then talked to me in gentle terms
Amidst the desert hush.

"Don't be afraid. I'll be your guide,
And it will all make sense.
Just follow me," and saying that,
He passed on through the fence.

His easy smile and beck'ning hand
Motioned me what to do.
Taking a long cold-water step,
I followed him on through.

We walked the whispering avenues,
Talking of way back when,
And listened to the women speak
Of their great need for men.

Well, that night their prayers were answered;
I saw it come to pass.
Dry grass became concrete once more,
All stained with oil and gas.

Ground crews clustered around their birds,
Readying them for flight,
And down the line came those of lore,
To get some time that night.

Stopped by an old B-24,
My friend said, "Want some fun?
Fly the right seat with me tonight,
Out on a Guernsey run."

We rushed our preflight, made our checks;
She was no hangar queen,
But joined late at Bunker Beacon,
So flew as Green Sixteen.

The approving air around us
Was filled with those reborn.
I knew the joy of men with wings,
Sounding the hunter's horn.

A bulky, dog-eared short snorter,
I signed with leaky pen,
A brotherhood unknown to most,
Yet prized by flying men.

In tight formation, through the night,
Field-grader moon above,
And happiness, that special pride,
Call it a kind of love.

But on landing came the sadness,
These times were all too rare,
We taxied to the parking ramp,
And chocks that spelled despair.

We walked the quiet avenues,
And watched them fade away.
Heads bowed and leather jacket backs,
With nothing more to say.

Concrete became dry grass once more,
The night wind moaned its loss.
I thought of brave men gone before,
A hat, a ring, a toss.

We reached the fence; I passed on through,
And saw a dead star swoon.
One slow salute and he walked back
Into his chain-link tomb.

* * * *

My alarm clock buzzed the morning;
I smiled myself awake.
I should have taken an extract,
Just for my form 5's sake.

Funny how real a fantasy
Based on dreams can become.
But I cut myself while shaving,
I had an ink-stained thumb.

The more technical among you can rightly take me to task about this ode. For several reasons, I decided to call it an ode. When I was in North Vietnam, no one knew what an ode was so it didn't make any difference, and I needed one anyway just to round out the collection. In any event, the T-33, that fine aircraft, should have this ode in its past, as well as the other skeletons.

Ode to a T-Bird

O T-Bird, noble aircraft, timeworn true,
Fair ramply fixture gracing every base,
Now lost within, as you have traveled through
The vast immensity of time and space.
And who shall feeling call thy sainted name,
Now that thy service lifespan finally done?
And where remembered resting place and fame?
A common grave beneath the desert sun.
Yet if of ere a nosewheel has been cocked,
A bucket blown or bulky seat pack sore,
As sure as thy J-8 has precessed locked,
Extended be thy presence evermore.
So long I hold, there be parts-pickup hops,
Somewhere, a T-Bird's parked in front of OPS.

Sonnet for Winged* Man

The amber-throated days of summer run
A single race, surprising short to fall.
Old passions mellow with the cooling sun,
And rising smoke from burning leaves a wall.
Though tender held, the shawl of autumn slips
And bares the trees to mufflered winter cold.
No more on placid ponds the painted ships,
To leeward helm bound home with weathered gold.
Yet if the fleeting season short for some,
For winged man more cruel the second hand,
With final landing logged will winter come
To icy grip, now shackled to the land.
But till last storm, he'll wait the banshee cry,
Run quick to look, his heart still in the sky.

* Pronounced wing´id

Friendship

A friend is a wingman.
A friend can be lead.
A friend is there when there's a need.

Who Is It?

Who is it sits in summer sun,
With air conditioner that won't run?
Who is it chill now winter come?
The heating unit on the bum.

Who is it sits with propped-up boot,
In salt-encrusted flying suit?
Who is it smokes fag after fag,
And reads the latest flying mag?

Who is this man who talks so crude?
The chosen one, grease pencil screwed.
Who is this chap who seldom speaks,
Yet monitors so many freqs?

Who is he not caught unawares
With loaded Very pistol flares?
The coffee drunk lukewarm and black,
By him who logs 'em off and back.

By now you've guessed our mystery friend,
If you've pulled time at runway's end.
That yellow box on wheels still waits
For you, perhaps, or squadron mates.

So watch some grease, some barely hack
A landing that would break your back,
But what the hell, they all got gear.
Thanks be to thee, dear mobileer.

This One Is for the Birds (Cross Country)

*(Use a Southern accent and syncopate
in latter portion of line.)*

Well, way down south on the Texas flat,
Where prickle pear and jackrabbit at,
Lived two woodpeckers in a sawed-off stump,
A-lookin' all the day for sumpin' to thump.

Now, I know'd one, name of Maggie Mo;
T'other buddy be B'rer Jamie Jo.
Maggie were IP with a bunch of rrrs,
But Jamie, he were young, kinda unawarrrs.

It happened one day as I recollect,
Setting on a cholla with nothing to peck,
Maggie turned to Jamie: "Say, brother-o,
I got me an idee think you oughta know.

"From yonder back, north to San Anton,
Local flyin' wood's dry as a bone.
Cottonwood, willer, other thorny thing
Just don't fill the bill, that empty holler ring.

"But I heard tell of a promised land,
Where trees grow tall and the peckin's grand.
Californy redwood, supposed to be best;
I be of a mind to mosey on out west."

Well, Jamie chawed, pondered it a spell;
It twern't too long he opined, "Do tell.
Maggie, what you say surely do appeal;
Guess I'll tag along, give them redwoods a feel."

The two ambled down, RAYDOE base ops;
Howdy to a few plannin' their hops.
They checked with weather, then into the charts,
Filed an eyeball route and departed them parts.

Maggie was a-leadin', first leg high,
Jamie on the wing, hanging right spry.
Fast as a possum clawin' up a tree,
The two headed west, flight level twenty-three.

Couple hours out they let on down;
Quick stop at Kirtland for turnaround.
Moon pie and cola, 'nother tank of gas,
Soon headed west again, really hauling . . . fas'.

Oak Creek Canyon, real purty passed by;
Jamie thrashing weeds, Maggie stacked high.
The two skedaddled in their feathered flight,
Pleased as Mr. Bullfrog on a moonlit night.

Round about Vegas, Maggie took lead.
Off to the west, some weather he seed.
"Hello there, Center, need a clearance now.
Dog, but that dark stuff sure bring sweat to the brow."

The two smoked on, undercast below;
Maggie said, "Boy, just a piece to go."
And sho nuff ahead, them big trees of red,
Where a fool could peck his brains out, till he dead.

They entered into holding by and by,
Weather mite touchy to Maggie's eye.
"We better take a TACAN, radar too.
Caution be the watchword, 'fore we have a chew."

Jamie started frettin', young and bold.
Called for clearance, "Continue to hold."
Jamie so bothered, so anxious to peck,
He rolled to his back and Split S'd to the deck.

Luck of a rebel helped him down.
Landed on a tree, commenced to pound,
He'd jest reared back for that first giant peck,
When come bolt of lightning, struck him in the neck.

Poor ole Jamie, layin' in the brush,
Tail feathers singed and a deathly hush.
Maggie was on final; he touched down good,
To a fine full stop next a likely hunk of wood.

Maggie looked for Jamie, peered to be,
Big Daddy Sherman had marched to the sea.
There were feathers all strewed, blood on the ground;
Jamie lay a-pantin' like a redbone hound.

Maggie stood a-lookin', shook his head.
"It's wonder, I declare, you ain't dead.
Now, I seed me some sights and heard me some tales,
There is one thing I know that's true for all males."

"Boy, 'fore you fly gen, think on these words.
It's true for man, and it's true for birds:
No matter what you call it, love or sin,
Don't be such a hurry, put your pecker in."

Weather Day

The APM drags snail-like on,
While cooling coffee turns to clay.
From Spang and Bitt to plateaued Hahn,
It's just another weather day.

The normal conversation gone,
In turn, each briefer has his say.
Response from slumping jocks, a yawn;
It's just another weather day.

A time for details to attend,
Till finally OPS decides a stay,
And scraping chairs declare the end;
It's just another weather day.

The snack bar fills with bets and brags,
And for a time some mild horseplay,
Then TAC Attack and other mags;
It's just another weather day.

The schedule board marked CNX,
Its names and planes in dim display,
Plus finger sketch, thus one reflects,
It's just another weather day.

Grey metal claims the shredded scraps,
As locker cleaning does away
With long-flown routes and penciled maps;
It's just another weather day.

Time-using tasks at length complete,
The weathered ones in green array
Go wandering halls on tethered feet;
It's just another weather day.

These hooded days, time seems to stall,
As airspeed and ideas stray.
Dash ones and target study call;
It's just another weather day.

The briefing room is filling slow;
The there-I-was types all dismay.
But still and all it's pretty slow;
It's just another weather day.

And unattended, put to bed,
Beneath a coverlet of grey,
The aircraft wait till once more wed;
It's just another weather day.

Now, you've been there and so have I,
Dull briefing room in disarray,
The careless legs and talk belie,
It's just another weather day.

If you're like me, then sure you know
These are the days we earn our pay.
The scenes the movies never show;
Yeah, just another weather day.

Carpet of Clouds

A recent PIREP calls it topping out,
Flight level twenty-two,
With CBs building, northwest quad,
Some anvil tops in view.

And so it is, as I come piercing through,
Abandoned grey and gauge,
To stride with giant steps upon
A great and vacant stage.

Gold flecked, extend a carpet wisping white
Beyond the eye and mind.
Here distant towering pillars stand
In warning to our kind.

I level scanning maybe six above;
My mask conceals a smile.
All mine, I climb, then half roll off
To Cuban 8 a mile.

My flashing craft alive to eager touch,
Responds with easy g.
We dive and zoom, then lazy roll,
A-skimming, running free.

A quick cross-check, my wandering mind attends,
As swept-back silver soars
Across the domed and vaulted heights
Along wide, wind-washed shores.

A pilot's halo follows fast beneath,
And boundless, like the air.
The joy of flight, though strapped in tight,
I find great freedom there.

Perhaps, below, some hapless soul can hear,
Faint bugles in the sky.
He'll shake his head at dark'ning clouds,
And wonder why we fly.

His collar up and cap pulled warding down,
He'll never know the thrill
Of chasing cross a shouting sky,
The solitude, the still.

But you've been there, so know of what I speak,
The empty spaces hurled.
From cockpit throne, you reign alone,
On top in Titan world.

Now marking on the antiseptic blue,
This message from the high,
Engraved within the hearts of men,
Who love and live to fly.

On top, some special sun-split afternoon,
You'll find no-limit sky,
And live lifetimes in brief minutes,
Whole lifetimes as you fly.

Life Flight
Leg #1

The active taken, how the runway seems
To vanish in the distant dawning light.
An AB roar before this world of dreams,
How final checks and takeoff roll excite.
Now running down the track, I do so much,
While great events like tumbling jackknives flash,
As panels pass, white panels pass, and touch
Of knowing hand directs departure dash.
Cleaned up and outbound now, the flight-planned route
Provides for challenge with success. And who
Cross-checks those gauges, will he execute
According to the hopes before he flew?
Well, he has wings, imparted IP skill;
Though takeoff roll be short, it should fulfill.

Leg #2

The first leg low, this longest leg of all,
My cockpit warm. Rich land a speeding mirth
Where color whips and blends a windswept shawl
Across the shouldered form of Mother Earth.
From lathered loins important issues spring,
Uncommon love and knowledge known complete.
The clarity that righteous cause can bring,
Until accumulation needs compete.
External tanks are blinking; time to switch.
On main. I mental note it's cost me some,
Can confidence discern a change in pitch?
It's charactered ambition that must come.
Ah yes, it's fun a-running fast and low;
Sometimes it's hard to pick up checkpoints, though.

Leg #3

Now intermediate in altitude,
A tailwind helps this longest second part.
Well-managed fuel and blue horizons viewed;
Detail concerns procedures known by heart.
A solitary introspection leads
Across variety of midday space.
Reporting points are timely called, but needs
Of binding metal loudly call home base.
A firm assurance leaves no room for doubt;
Continue, reinforcement undenied
Protects us both from bitter cold without.
That special warmth of inner faith and pride.
Remember, not all take the chosen route,
There's targets you will lose, despite pursuit.

Leg #4

It's shortly after midday that I change
To positive control perspective plane.
Though certain satisfaction isn't strange,
Complacency earns shoddy flying gain.
I detour weather, thanks to radar guide;
He helps me through the buildups troubling some.
Sincerely I have laughed, sincerely cried,
Of course, and pity them with feelings numb.
By star, DR, and beacon, steering well.
Compete against myself and testing too
The deeds I've done and those I'll do, I tell
The sky, my love, my estimation true.
This long, rewarding leg requires toil,
But happy he who knows both sky and soil.

Leg #5

High altitude, the structure of white clouds
Above lends majesty to measured gait.
Below, so far removed the rushing crowds,
And I find great contentment with my state.
I think about the wingmen I have sought
To value and be valued in return,
And if I've learned a bit, I've also taught,
What lessons fair experience can earn.
I talk to old friend center as before,
His monitor and guidance through my flight,
Yet forecast of assurance comforts more,
As destination nears with coming night.
I ramble some, although my track be straight,
On course, on time, reviewing let down plate.

Leg #6

I teardrop leave the final holding fix,
And yet so keen anticipate my task.
Precise and firm as joy and sorrow mix,
This last approach will penetrate the mask.
On top my contrails linger like all men.
Brief monuments, they span the east and west,
Then quickly fade against time's racing pen.
Short hop 'bout done, record, I've flown my best.
Controlled, come home, long runway beck'ning crown.
A final flare to gentle ground, I roll
Past panels, think of panels, braking down,
And know a pleasant weariness of soul.
Slow taxi now, to rest a little while.
The final marker, turn off, I can smile.

The Loneliest Place in Town

How many chill and pitchlike nights,
Amidst soft drizzling from the scud,
Has my hand extinguished headlights,
Boots crunching gravel, eyes I rub.

The tower beacon fending fair
In battle 'gainst the airy deep,
Its green-white gaze a passing stare
Above a line that lies asleep.

Blue fingers stretch beyond the ramp
That garners those in resting row,
Awaiting man and morning lamp
To spread their wings and plumage show.

Dull echo from the wooden stoop
And scuffed linoleum timeworn.
Do not disturb dispatcher troop
On Army cot this early morn.

Pale night-light glow, faint wreath behind
The duty desk, its phones and forms,
Of which just two my fingers find,
Designed to guide through sun and storms.

The wall clock clicks, near half past three,
Command post answers with a yawn.
Route info and a hack for me,
About to leap in dark predawn.

Top marred and rubbed from years of use,
The elbows and the countless hands,
With supplements and charts profuse,
The darkened planning table stands.

A single hanging bulb provides
A poolroom glow. I take my cue,
And go with addict-driven strides
For vended coffee, lifeblood brew.

Machine-made caffeine pick-me-up
Renews within the inner man.
I steadfast clutch the warming cup
And briefly, yellow NOTAMs scan.

I thumb reports historical,
Then take my weather brief by phone
From sleepless Norton oracle,
Pen scratching to his knowing drone.

More coffee and a cigarette,
Computing quick in standard rite.
It's fuel and time, my distance set,
The math parameters of flight.

I spin and jot, then double-check;
My weather check is two plus ten.
A solo recce T-Bird trek
For TAC-deploying brother men.

I gently rouse the airman third;
He springs to stockinged foot alert.
And so I file with cheerful word
My try to ease the wak'ning hurt.

I go to gather gear in back,
His words to center eremite:
"Departure, speed, flight level, track,
Then home to George around first light."

Pale night-light glow doth regs appease,
As I return the room so dim,
A seat pack slapping at my knees
The only sound save huddled him.

I pause to snub a cigarette,
While scanning tired walls and floor
And wondering how their courses set
The old and bold ones gone before.

The wall clock clicks; it's now near four.
The night and damp'ning ramp await.
I hike my chute and shut the door,
Off once again to live my fate.

Behind a crumpled monument
As night-light shadows start to creep,
My passing marked, concomitant,
Base Operations sound asleep.

Soon there comes a whine in warning,
No need to tell if you've been down.
Base Ops at four in the morning,
It's the loneliest place in town.

The Ballad of the
Cross-Country Flyer

He wore a big hack watch and fighter-pilot boots;
He was liquored, he was leathered, he was lean.
He'd RON'd at Nellis, drank, gambled, chased the toots;
He was outbound now, all gauges green.

His visor down and slumpin', great gulps of oxygen;
He's so hurtin', he's so haggard, he's so hung.
With bloodshot blivet eyes and a pickle-tasting tongue,
He's filed direct and BLD is swung.

East of Tuba City storm clouds start to build,
So somewhere 'bout mid-canyon, he pushes up to mil.
He's only got an ugly hog, many has it thrilled;
Upward losing airspeed, feeling kinda ill.

Now standing on his tailpipe, just barely in the clear,
He's frantic callin' center, requesting weather steer.
But center doesn't answer, and C sub L max near.
He stalls and spins that mother; "Oh Shit and Oh Dear."

Dark clouds all around him, aircraft that won't fly;
"Lord oh Lord, be with me," his graveyard spiral cry.
"I'll never lay another bet, on that you can rely.
Just kick a little rudder, Lord; I'm too young to die."

"Now, all you disbelievers take note of what I say,
I was in the cockpit that dark and gruesome day.
I can't describe what happened; there isn't any way.
But I snapped to straight and level and continued on OK."

Still dark and heavy weather, I pressed on zero nine,
A-talking, squawking center, faint hoping sun would shine.
Then came some buzz-saw static and a high-pitched piercing whine;
A moment later, headset dead, I'm NORDO off the line.

Not satisfied, misfortune kept dealing heavy blows;
The TACAN started spinnin', my compass card, it froze.
With circuit breakers poppin', adding to my woes,
Oil smoke started seeping up between my toes.

The fire light was flashing, EGT beserk;
Hydraulic pressure zero, another minor irk.
RPM unwinding, it hung up with a jerk.
Enough for me. I tried my seat; the bastard didn't work.

"Lord oh Lord, it's me again, same old luckless guy,
In need of major maintenance, sir, so this bird'll fly.
I'll never take another drink, no more rock and rye.
I'm off the booze, it's up to you, will I live or die?"

There I was at thirty thou, my situation tough.
Once more the old man in the sky put me on the cuff;
The Christmas tree extinguished, he really did his stuff.
Soon flying smooth, point seven two; I guess I paid enough.

I drove on uneventful, tailwinds, making hay,
Commencing letdown sixty out, direct to GCA.
The field was holding just above minimums that day;
I vectored down through layers where embedded CU did lay.

Leaving twelve and calling, so far still shooting scratch,
I bend her up in rounding a rather fearsome batch.
I get too close and now it's gross, that bumper makes a snatch;
I find myself a-fringing through a fairly hairy patch.

But low at two I spot some blue; an opening does cajole.
OK, you single-saddle steed, let's make like a mole.
On I flew, got halfway through, the boiler full of coal.
Blue turned to black; I've had the cack: it's just a sucker hole.

The inside of a thousand, be they witches or whate'er,
And me bowel boring deeper through that fulsome-odored lair;
I felt someone a-plucking at my short and private hair.
The aircraft started bucking; things ripped beyond repair.

First scraping from the canopy, then floorboard bound for thrills,
How well do I remember those violent whifferdills.
The stick is ineffective, indifferent to my skills;
The aircraft starts to tumble and my lunch bag spills.

I tunneled in almost blacked, excessive g oppressed,
Rivets poppin' swappin' ends, my bladder overstressed.
My weekend-warrior weakened heart clumping in my breast,
Once more I turned my thoughts upstairs; this was the final test.

"Lord oh Lord, how could you? Affirmative, 'tis I,
Here I come on bended wing, cartwheeling through the sky.
I've one last vow to offer, just get me through my cry,
And no more bed until I'm wed, no more rubbing thigh."

The collection plate was sagging, passing round the pews.
There you have it, now sworn off gambling, broads, and booze.
Image tender throttle benders say better life to lose,
That's verbal varnish, armor tarnished, nicked and scratched I choose.

My requisition chit was in; would it be approved?
The clerk at distribution really must have moved,
For sudden in a blinding flash, erratic flight was smoothed.
Thin and tranquil, breaking up, the angry heavens soothed.

My trim tabs kiss the clouds good-bye, home plate below not far.
I drop my nose to entry point, CAVU to nearest star.
I hit the break and things are jake so stand her on the spar,
Then button G and as I key, my words of thanks they are,
"You can cancel out that clearance, Lord. I'm downwind VFR."

Section II

POW and Other "Dark and Bitter Stuff"

Question: *"What was it like up there?"*

Answer: *"There were optimists and pessimists. The pessimists thought that we would die up there and they wouldn't even send our bodies home. The optimists were sure they would send our bodies home."*

"Yea, though I walk through the valley of the shadow of death I shall fear no evil because I am the toughest SOB in the valley." —**Fighter pilot bravado**

"The bells of hell will ring—ding-a-ding-ding— for you but not for me. Better days are coming by and by." —**Bar song**

The Tourney

The scepter raised and silent challenge made,
Again I mental summon lance and shield,
And somehow last till regal colors fade.
It's now, the victor absent from the field,
Hard pallet draws me, huddled down upon,
A distant tower tolls a muffled chime;
Another muddled day has eddied on
To join the addled streams of tousled time.
Embittered languor blankets captive man;
So armored, sally forth at dawn, consigned
To stand alone, and parry best I can
Until appointed tourney's end, resigned.
For time's an old and boring enemy.
Too cruel to kill forgotten men like me.

Beneath Thin Blanket

From huddled sleep, from humbled sleep,
My sickened shape awakes.
Still lost in darkness,
Beneath thin blanket.

Sick lungs suck deep, asthmatic deep,
It's cold, controlless shakes
Across the chamber,
Beneath thin blanket.

I struggle steep against the steep
Of loathsome life that breaks
The sure and sureless,
Beneath thin blanket.

I'll fight till sleep, till tired sleep
My sickened shape retakes.
Still lost in darkness,
Beneath thin blanket.

The Carnival

Come ride the gaily colored carrousel;
A golden ring awaits the agile hand.
The barker's voice and music swell;
Best hurry or you'll have to stand.

So join the headless crowd in bargain shove,
The laughter gay and price in pennies cheap.
Bright bathed in glitter from above,
Mount up for fun with frenzied leap.

A-whirling then on gaudy painted steed,
Around and round atop the sawdust slush.
But few the precious circuits heed
Till worn gears grate, then grinding . . . hush.

"One ride per customer," the crone intones;
She cackles as the wide-eyed disembark.
The midway dims with patrons' groans;
Soft sawdust deeper now, and dark.

The carny's closed, its crass allurement gone;
Deserted horses clad in canvas tombs.
The dirt, the smells, a greased tarp drawn
On derelicts with futile brooms.

Hanoi Epitaph

When days of dim hope and boredom abound,
And you half listen to the desperate sound
Of empty tap-code conversation.

When the heat is so hot, and cold so cold,
You think of your youth and how you've grown old,
The endless and senseless frustration.

When things don't go right and treatment is bad,
You think of the war and how you've been had,
Now live confined; it's life's lowest station.

When you try to do the job expected,
"Hang on, keep faith," till resurrected,
Without plaudit or praise from the nation.

When you cling to values you know are true,
Like family, God, the red, white, and blue,
It's your fortress 'gainst indoctrination.

When floodwaters rise, breaking mind levee,
You go on, though the standard staff heavy,
But you live in confirmed desperation.

When the floor is furrowed by tired feet,
And life slips away 'neath the pounding beat,
You trudge on, in the dark desolation.

When years have passed, the many Decembers,
And no one cares and no one remembers
The lost flyer and his supplication.

When the bombing has stopped with no end in sight,
Cover your ears as we cry in the night,
With considerable justification.

When you can't go on, the burden too great,
And words lose their meaning, except the word "hate,"
You bend and forget repatriation.

The man on the street, a face in the crowd,
Isn't concerned with the mind-numbing shroud
That grey time causes us to be lost in.

The years have passed, the many Decembers,
And no one knows and no one remembers
The sound of your voice, your face, or your name.

So you dream of steel chargers, skies to roam;
Mostly you dream of . . . just going home.
But you dream without hope or conviction.

The Road

A field and a fence, then the winding road.
A narrow, nameless nothing of a road.
Sometimes in the day, travel some by light.
Mostly in the dark, darkness of the night.

Then come the trucks, grinding up the track,
Jolting, jarring, olive muddy black.
Past the wounded field, past the twisted gate,
Running east to dawn; dawn is always late.

The road rests, resting, shoulder humbled down;
Drizzle spits, muck shifts, drizzle draining down.
Tired like a whore, known too many men;
Tired asking why, tired asking when.

Now it's Jim Joe John Jack, pack upon his back,
Marching, marching, never looking back.
Frightened he's afraid, frightened that he's brave;
Marching to the front, marching to his grave.

The track and the tread numbered days record.
The road remains, remains to be ignored.
Engineer, regard your road, work in vain.
To make crooked straight and rough places plain.

Sonnet 4 45 43
(In tap code) Sonnet for Us

The world without, within our weathered walls,
Remote, like useless windows, small and barred.
Here, months and years run quickly down dim halls,
But days, the daze, the empty days come hard.
I used to count a lot, count everything,
Like exercise and laps and words of prayer.
What hurt that hunger, thoughts that thirst can bring,
Companions, waking, sleeping, always there.
But policy insanities unwind,
Till bad is good and betterment is worse.
So refuge blanket, net, and molding mind
Create a mingling dream-real universe.
I'm told that steel is forged by heavy blows.
If only men were steel, but then, who knows?

Affliction and Predilection

I curse sore throats, raw rasping coats
Of thickening, rubbing phlegm.
No lozenge made or prayer prayed
Assists assuaging them.

Elastic spit, the rough, hot grit
When swallowing, and yet,
I curse the more, when though throat sore,
I smoke a cigarette.

On Love

O Love, would that thy flame unkept could burn,
Untended ever, while soft shadows dance.
Would thou consume and yet consuming, spurn,
Abating not to force perverse or chance.
If brilliance undiminished could conceal,
If appetite unnourished were content,
Then love should stand and challenge time to kneel,
And likely, trickling sand would cease unspent.
Despite vowed constancy and selflessness,
Love's but a greedy smile and tarnished eye,
Demanding soon a toil whose worthlessness
Is measured in exposure of the lie.
Examine effort, then, the murmured bile.
At best, you'll ward off cold a little while.

The Journey

An erring wind churns the high desert dust;
Alkaline lakes flash past the travel-dirtied car.
Weathered hands upon a wheel;
They know the work of planting time, the joy of harvest.
So many miles, so many thoughts,
So many miles.

They were helpful at the base, and the hand-drawn map,
The map . . . it's easy to follow.
Turning off the highway at a diner baking quietly in the midday sun
It's eight arrowlike miles of country road,
Country road to a lonesome low house
Squatting on the desert flat behind a taut barbed-wire fence.

The cattle-guard gate clangs arrival;
A medium mongrel dog sounds intruder
Till silenced by a spare, levied man.
Thinking no one can really understand,
You say the words that cause your journey.
Yet this stranger meets your eye and nods;
In the moment's silence, see yourself reflected.

You decline the traditional coffee and offer of his truck.
You have to walk.
You'll need the time, both going and returning.

Three-quarters of a mile,
Across a waste of shrub and Joshua tree embedded in the sand.
Each step a step of penance across the greying soil,

For memories long forgotten, like tucking in the bed,
Dreams all clouded over, and things that went unsaid.
Far back recall the last time that you kissed;
After that, just a hug or two and you shook hands instead.

The land cries out for water,
Lips cracked with endless thirst.
O give me life, let greenery grow,
And at my breast be nursed.

You see it now, the wounded land,
A scar that rips the ground.
An ugly slash that ends it all,
And emptiness is found.

Approach the lacerated earth
Stand numb and hear the roar,
A silver bird's great dying dance
Upon this valley floor.

Walk down that swath to the scorched end,
This part so very hard.
Stare at the final resting place,
Where all your hopes are charred.

Stand on the spot and feel the scar
Of inner soul and sod,
No doctor's hand can mend or heal.
Just nature, time, and God.

Shade your eyes and look across the dry land;
Shade your eyes as they start to run.
Shade your eyes as your aching heart dies,
And mourn your only son.

Bury your hurt in blackened dirt;
Now done, your task is through.
Turn your back, go quickly away;
It's time to start anew.

You are glad the yard is empty;
Even the dog is gone.
So into the car and fast away,
Into a midday dawn.

But going slow along the road,
Allow one backward look.
Now see a worn and battered sign
That's fallen from its hook.

Broken, hand-lettered, it tells all,
Though you will never know,
The eulogy it speaks for him
And others who will go.

So on your way, let others heed
The time to them that's lent.
Yes, those who know the meaning of
"Farm Land for Sale or Rent."

Section III

The Holidays and Hollow Days

"The happy and the sad moments tore at the heart."
—John Borling

The Other Christmas

T'was the night before Christmas, and out at alert,
Not a creature was stirring, the TV inert.
The pilots and crew chiefs in bunk rooms asleep,
Toss, fitful, awaiting the klaxon to leap.
And off in the corner, a dark tinseled tree,
It's Christmas again in the land of the free.

T'was the night before Christmas, out over the pond,
Where a Starlifter strains for far Europe beyond.
The drone of its engines, an olde carol, say,
"Ramstein tomorrow, Adana next day."
Its instrument panel dull red all aglow,
Back home at McGuire, it's starting to snow.

T'was the night before Christmas, so far out at sea,
Be it cruiser, destroyer, or giant CV.
Up forward, the lookout marks tolling of bell;
No church steeples here, just salt spray and groundswell.
And on watch from on high, the OD doth roam,
The Captain's Chair empty, both here and at home.

T'was the night before Christmas, up over the Pole,
There's a B-52 on atomic patrol.
With peace their profession, its crew does attend
Their fortress of strength to deter and defend.
Strange, all electronics of this modern day
Show nary a sign of old Santa and sleigh.

T'was the night before Christmas, deployment call comes,
So good-bye, little children who dream sugarplums.
Tomorrow they'll wake, their young eyes all alight,
Then blink back the tears, Daddy's left in the night.
Now far from the hearth where each stocking is hung
Cross cold, starlit skies, a small aircraft is flung.

T'was the night before Christmas, down deep in the pad
Stands a Minuteman poised, if the world should go mad.
Its cold chimney silo hath no warming place,
Nor rooftop awaiting a swift courser's pace.
And what yuletide missal from men waiting still,
Though strange it may seem, peace on earth, and goodwill.

T'was the night before Christmas, mud up to the knee;
There's a lone foxhole dug by a young PFC.
He's only eighteen; Christmas Eve seems to close.
But ready he stands, to destroy unknown foes.
He's scared, but he'll do the grim job that he must,
In him, have you placed your defense and your trust.

T'was the night before Christmas, all over this earth;
There's a serviceman standing, no mistletoe mirth.
He's Army and Navy, Air Force and Marines;
If asked, he could tell you how much Christmas means.
You don't know his name, waiting children or wife,
But for you, if need be, he'll lay down his life.

T'was the night before Christmas, and then Christmas Day,
And just maybe, you'll think of those men far away.
And just maybe, take out a moment or two,
Say a short prayer for them, the family, and you.
A small price indeed for your bright, tinseled tree,
It's Christmas again in the land of the free.

Mommy, Where Is My Daddy?

I hear you walking in the night;
You think I'm fast asleep.
I know your sounds of loneliness;
I hear you pray and weep.

You think that I'm too young to know
The agony and pain
Of missing the man gone away
In search of war and fame.

He didn't come home with all the rest;
It's been four years and more.
His squadron mates don't know his fate,
O cruel, unending war.

I try to fill the gap he's left,
For emptiness adjust.
I love him though he's just a dream,
And picture that we dust.

Oh Mommy, where is my daddy?
Won't he ever be coming home?
You say he loves us so very much,
But he's left us so long alone.

* * * *

Lauren, my precious daughter,
This tale you must be told.
Your daddy wore the silver wings
Of Air Force pilots bold.

He loved the world of speed and sound;
He flew the Phantom Two.
And life was love and freedom's fight;
What happiness we knew.

He told me before we married,
About his other life,
And how he wanted me to be
A loyal Air Force wife.

At times I hated those four words,
But did the best I could.
I know he loved me all the more,
Because I understood.

You'd have to see the look he wore
When coming in at night.
A hug, a kiss, and then his words:
"Gee, I had a great flight."

He'd tell us of the wondrous things
He'd seen and done that day.
Aloft in his great chariot,
Holding the world at bay.

He'd play with you and fool with me,
Out on the front-room floor.
Then talk about a pot of gold
And rainbow he did score.

But now he's gone, listed missing,
Ten thousand miles away.
And nothing left for us to do,
Just sit and wait and pray.

He will be coming home one day,
Believe with all your heart.
He'll laugh and hold us in his arms,
And time again will start.

* * * *

Myrna and Lauren, my darlings,
The hurt I've caused to you.
It pains me more than my sad fate,
For nothing I can do.

The endless days have turned to years;
Impossible, it seems.
And all our plans and all our hopes
Are now just shattered dreams.

Honey, they've just about killed it,
The drive and the desire
To make my mark and get ahead.
Just embers now, no fire.

I know that I must fly again,
Be free and know the joy,
As boundless skies and purest air
Help memories destroy.

I know that I must love again,
My child and faithful wife.
The dim-bright figures of my past,
The touchstones of my life.

I seek elusive happiness,
That most men never know.
To be in love with home and work,
And help my country grow.

And God must play a vital part;
To him all thanks belong.
For he is here when I am weak,
And helps me get along.

Still, I run an uncertain race.
Ahead, another bend.
My breath comes short and I'm so worn,
Not sure if there's an end.

I think of small things like front doors,
Rooms with familiar chairs,
Recollections, I long to see,
And you upon the stairs.

But now I'm gone, listed missing,
Ten thousand miles away.
And nothing left for me to do,
Just sit and wait and pray.

I will be coming home one day;
Believe with all your heart.
I'll hold you in my arms and . . . try to laugh,
And time again will start.

Excerpt from a Christmas Letter*

And how I've sought that special thought
With meaning just for you.
The memories shared, how dreams have fared,
The things that we will do.

But how to tell, what feelings well,
What message to impart?
Perhaps, dear wife, just "You're my life";
So beats my constant heart.

* *A Christmas letter of the mind, as there was no mail for many years.*

A Part of Christmas

When Jack Frost starts a-warming hearts
And old man Smith ain't mean,
When reindeer fly and you can buy
A purple evergreen,
Then something's up, and you know what?
It's all a part of Christmas.

Snow tires crunch, it's Field's for lunch,
The window-shopping's grand.
Street-corner crush and friendly rush
Through downtown wonderland,
Where bells are rung and carols sung.
It's all a part of Christmas.

While wallets strain and feet complain,
Department stores go mad.
The things to buy, a youngster's cry,
"I just saw Santa, Dad.
He said, 'Be good.' I said I would."
It's all a part of Christmas.

Last-minute gifts and plowed-up drifts,
Galoshes trudging through.
Can you believe it's Christmas Eve
With nothing left to do?
The car door slams; we're off to Gram's.
It's all a part of Christmas.

Grandfather's smile, the present pile,
A treetop angel there.
So family met and table set,
All heads now bow in prayer.
"OK, dig in," again the din.
It's all a part of Christmas.

There's turkey, hams, and candied yams;
Sage dressing hits the spot.
The lingon's great; my gosh, my plate
Can really hold a lot.
More pumpkin pie, I'll probably die.
It's all a part of Christmas.

Well, Santa comes, the kids all thumbs,
Home movies blind us all.
Gift paper flies, white shirts and ties,
Skates rumble down the hall.
A car key search and off to church.
It's all a part of Christmas.

The message told, both young and old
Rejoice the Christ Child's birth.
The meaning real as church bells peal
A prayer for peace on earth.
And then, "Good night, drive safe, sleep tight."
It's all a part of Christmas.

* * * *

It's later now; remember how
Old street lamps used to shine?
The shoveled walks, our quiet talks,
Your mittened hand in mine.
A wintry kiss, my frosty miss,
That too a part of Christmas.

Yes, later now, imagine how
That front-yard snowman fares.
The porch is swept, house looks well kept,
So, slowly, climb the stairs.
A wreath, a door, they're waiting for
A needed part of Christmas.

The way is blocked, the door is locked,
A rough wind rakes the snow.
And almost there, that home, somewhere,
What will a window show?
Through patterned panes, a scene explains
Another part of Christmas.

A Scotch pine trimmed, the room is dimmed,
Few pillows here and there,
And by the tree, my darling be,
Her sad and pensive air.
"Remember, hon, the winter fun?"
So much a part of Christmas.

She kneels beside a package tied,
Bright ribbons and a bow.
Her fingers graze the paper's glaze
And glistening eyes may show
How many more are waiting for
Her missing part of Christmas.

The moments drag, old memories nag,
If only he were here.
The need to write this Christmas night
And feel a little near.
A lonely wife, a half a life,
And this, a part of Christmas.

It's Christmas Eve. Our little girl is long ago in bed—exhausted but happy. As usual, we had dinner and all with the folks but came home early, right after church. I'm sitting by the tree now, our stereo playing softly, and I feel very close to you. When I tucked our daughter in bed, she asked, "Mommy, will Daddy be home next Christmas?" I hope so, my darling, but always remember your little family is waiting, and we love you.

The Crying Part of Christmas

* * * *

Somewhere there's snow, a beacon glow,
It's just a window light.
A little spark that braves the dark,
It calls us home tonight.
A world away, return someday,
And be a part of Christmas.

Reflection

A golden ladle dips in the western sky,
An evening breeze gentles fir trees high.
The plain song of a nest-bound bird grows dim.
Think of places been, those to roam.
And now, far away, think of home.

This I Believe

Some are made for mountains,
Some prefer the plain,
But each must have self-esteem
To bring him home again.

Values come from people,
Assessing their amounts.
Those worthy of respect and pride,
All know the striving counts.

Tomorrow

If a word could express mutual stress
Over the long empty years,
It would have to include continual mood,
Frustrated hopes, and the tears
For mistakes of the past; and in order to last,
Credible promise appears.

And the word does exist; now mentally twist
Under its burden again.
From the devil's own deep, its meaning we keep.
Murmur it low and pretend
Tomorrow will come, word like a star,
On distant dim light depend.

It's tomorrow today; unusual way
Time seems to stop and then start.
At this moment I pause, my reason because
Yesterday calls my young heart.
I must mend and replace, cross life's open space,
Word tools essential, in part.

You supported the flag, and though we won't brag,
Quietly pleased and so proud,
Add my thanks and respect, for you did elect
Waiting, as faithfully vowed.
And my queen raised alone princess Lauren, who's shown
Beauty and grace you've endowed.

There is more we can glean from yesterday's scene;
Marriage is placed on the scales.
And the balance is bad, though good that we had,
Satisfied, somehow it pales.
When with perfection compared, I see I have erred;
Now for correction details.

Yes, tomorrow today, not future delay;
Life will be lived like a flame.
Our just recompense, it burns white intense,
Summoning fortune and fame.
On an end we begin, and the prize we shall win
Happiness, ours to reclaim.

The Virtue of a Snowball

"Yo, Eddie. Yo, Eddieee."
Chew and swallow, chew and swallow pea-potatoes. Chew
and swallow gravy bread and meat and milk and gulp and,
"Can I be excused, please?"
"Wipe your mouth."
"But?"
"Push in your chair. Don't run."

* * * *

The threshold is a thousand leagues away. A league's a . . .
an awful lot, and anyway I'm there and run.
"WALK."—And walk.

I like the front closet. It has smooth walls and smells so swell,
And cap and coat, earmuffs and mittens. I like gloves best,
but they always buy me mittens. That fur thing with
the heads is gonna bite somebody sometime . . . but it won't
bite me cuz I watch it.

"Yo, Eddie."
"GALOSHES." When I grow up, I'll never wear anything but
tennis shoes . . . but I won't buckle 'em.
SLAM!
"Yo, Eddie."
"Yo, how's the packin'?"
"Packin's good."
Clomp, clomp.
"Where's the guys?"
"Jimmy's gotta go to his sister's piano recital and Rol's going
to church again with his mom."

"Twice."

"Yeah, and he's gotta wear a suit too."

"Suits itch. If I made suits, I'd make 'em so they don't itch."

"Don't itch me."

"Say."

"Don't itch, cross my heart."

"Cross it. Well, they itch me."

"I got a trick. Wear pajamas under."

"Goll."

"Or you can wrap newspapers round your legs and rubber band 'em, but you crinkle when you walk. . . . jamas are better."

"Yo, Sammy. Yo, Sammeee."

WAIT.

"Betcha I can jump from the top step past the second crack."

"Aw."

"Betcha."

"Yo, Sa—"

"You boys go away now. Sammy can't come out."

"Why not, Miz Cavanaugh? Can we come in?"

"No, no, you just go away. Sammy has to stay in."

Clomp, clomp.

"He's in Dutch. Probably his sister did it. Why's a guy gotta have a sister, anyway?"

"I got a sister. She's OK . . . sometimes. Her boyfriend plays center and has a convertible and gives me quarters."

"Why?"

"Dunno. I guess to stay away when he's kissing her."

"He does?"

"Yeah, but he plays center, and—"

"Goll, I'll never do that. . . . You?"

"Nah, not me."

Clomp, clomp.
"I got two sisters. I'm in the middle. I can scare the littlest with Mom's fur thing, but the big one thinks she's big and her report cards are A's but I can tickle her. She hits me and I can't punch back cuz she's a girl. I did once, though, and got a tannin' with the hairbrush."
"Hurt?"
"Uh-huh . . . but once we were making each other dizzy and I let her go when we were spinning and she hit her head on the table and got knocked out. Mom was on the phone and she dropped it and started crying but Sis woke up and had a lump for a week. It turned all sorts of colors even though they put a knife on it and ice too."
"You get another tannin'?"
"No . . . and it must have hurt more than a sock."
Clomp, clomp.
"Where we gonna build the fort?"
"I dunno. How 'bout the park?"
"Ah, the big kids skating'll wreck it, and—"
"Yeah. . . . School?"
"School?"
"No—not school".
"Hey, let's put it on the hills by the tracks and then we can get 'em comin' up the hills and boxcars too. OK?"
"K by me."
Clomp, clomp. Clomp, clomp.

* * * *

Building forts on hills is hard work . . . man's work. Building, rolling, packing, stacking snow. Snow means blue, cold fingers, a runny nose, and tingling toes on radiators after cocoa in the kitchen after building.

* * * *

"Eddie, where do all the trains go? I bet they go everywhere."
"Guess so. Two weeks ago we went to Wallacetown to see Grandma and had a flat on the hill. There was a train there too. Men were walking by the train swinging lanterns . . . big red lanterns, but all'cept one got on the train at the top of the hill and went away."
"What about the one that didn't?"
"He went into a little house that had smoke coming out of a chimney."
"Oh."
"Dad let me help change the tire. He said a word and Mom got mad."
"What'd he say?"
"Don't 'member, but he skinned his knuckle bad."
"I'm gonna have a lantern someday and make the trains stop and go."
"I'm gonna ride the trains."
"Not 'less I wave the lantern."
"You will . . . woncha?"
"Yeah, cuz you're my friend."
"You're my friend too. You wanna go?"
"How do you get back home? Wallacetown is—"
"Wallacetown. How 'bout Cleveland?"
"I've never been to Cleveland."
"Me neither."
"How high we gonna make it?"
"Just a little higher, cuz we want it best. It's gonna be our best one."
"It's awful big now."
"Wait till we finish and put up the flag. You'll see."
"But what if it warms up and melts?"
"It won't. It's gonna to last a long time."
"OK."
"See your breath?"
"Yeah."

"My uncle Harold smokes cigars and blows smoke rings."

"You can't do that with breath."

"He talks a lot and wants me to sit on his knee. I don't like to cuz I don't think he really wants me to. 'Sides, it's hard and I get smoke in my eyes."

"When you go see Santa, his lap is soft."

"Depends on the Santa, mostly."

"How come there's so many and only supposed to be one?"

"Helpers, that what Mom says."

"Oh. . . . You ever see the real one?"

"Nope. Heard him, though."

"Coming down the chimney?"

"We don't have a chimney."

"How's he get in?"

"We leave the front door unlocked, and last year I heard him come in and laugh and go out again."

"You didn't go down?"

"Mom said I had to go to bed and not get up till six."

"Did ya?"

"After I heard him go out, I got up and went to the landing and asked for a drink of water. I saw all the presents he'd just left and Mom and Dad looking at 'em. They let me come down and open one. You know my red dump truck? That's it. I had to go back to bed till morning and I took it with me. A wheel came off but Dad fixed it."

"Eddie, I don't think my sister believes in Santa Claus."

"Everyone believes in Santa Claus. Besides, my mom told me so, and moms never fib."

"How many snowballs we gonna make?"

"A bunch—gotta be ready."

Scoop and scrape and pack and pack and pack and stack and scoop and scrape and pack and pack and pack and stack in forts on hills along the track . . . in forts with flags on hills.

Below, the naked trees, their gnarling bent in comprehension long ago, observe and rattle in the wind. A winter wind that rises down dim streets and beats with darkness broken bricks and buildings . . . always building.

"Hey, Eddie?"
"Huh?"
"It's getting dark. I have to go home now or Mom'll be mad."
"Me too."
"It's a good fort."
"Best."
"What are we going to do with all the snowballs?"
"Save 'em. Use 'em tomorrow."
"No one will steal 'em?"
"Nobody steals snowballs."
Clomp, clomp.
"See ya, Eddie."
"See ya."
"You know, we didn't even—"
"Tomorrow. We did a lot today."
"Tomorrow. Well, good work."
"Good work."
Clomp, clomp. Clomp, clomp. Clomp, clomp.

* * * *

The world is dark, but wonderful with snow,
Bay windows helping cast their patterned glow
As small boys trudge home, slowly counting lights,
Their snowballs made and stacked to worthy heights.

Are men just little boys who need to grow
And learn of life, its adverse undertow?
More fair perhaps if men could lose grey years,
Recapture boyhood hopes and dreams and tears.

Deliberately along the track I go,
To watch the small boys working with their snow.
"Is the packin' good, and how far can you throw?"
There's virtue in a snowball we don't know.

Section IV

SEA Story
(Southeast Asia Story)

Epic poems are long and tell the story of heroic figures.
I wanted the challenge to create and keep
such a poem memorized.

This epic is inspired by men and many real-life events
from the Vietnam War, especially those who waged the
air war from Thailand. For all the many rest of you,
it's a great ride, so get into the glossary and
get grounded before we get airborne.

Southeast Asia Story

One WOXOF day,
Down Ubon way,
The monsoon rains in town,
Out at the base,
The 8th was in place,
But flying ops were down.
The wind was growling,
Jocks were lolling,
A weather day condition.
When holy smoke,
Some frags they broke,
Said we had a mission.

At hour eleventh,
The wing called seventh,
Advising we're no-go.
The word came back,
You'll be in hack;
The mission, it will go.
We'll lose our place
In the sortie race,
This battle just begun.
Not old Ho Chi
Or the DRV,
Beat Navy number one.

Some shoe clerks laughed
At the shaft
And started taking bets.
The flight crews scowled
As they howled
And muttered evil threats.
The pilots knew
That if they flew,
The clag would take its toll.
When you fly the pipe,
You take it in type;
No need to mention the hole.

Ops took the floor.
He called for four;
Four crews to volunteer.
He told a joke
As he spoke
And promised us free beer.
Hands went up slow,
A middling show,
We realized the need.
He bummed a light,
Then picked the flight
And chose himself as lead.

Scheduled ground spare,
The chance was fair
I would not be called upon.
Flight-planning away,
Cursing the day
I came to old Ubon.
To my disbelief,
The target brief
Showed some suspicious trees.
A suspected road
Would bear our load,
And bring them to their knees.

The colonel came in;
We said to him,
"For this we risk our ass?
To bomb some jungle,
What a bungle.
To hell with Mu Gia Pass."
"It should improve,"
He said real smooth;
We didn't believe a word.
"And I'll be along,
In spirit strong."
We flipped him the bloody bird.

At final brief,
The weather chief
Mumbled through lips half closed,
"The whole world's down.
So's Ubon town;
You guys are getting hosed.
The powers that be
Say you'll see
A hundred and a quarter.
I'm telling you
It isn't true;
The clag's as thick as mortar."

I watched lead smile;
I liked his style.
He told the sarge, "No sweat.
A little scary,
Not too hairy,
No need to get upset.
My flight will go
With an ITO,
Professionals all the way.
We'll Aqua-Lung
To Package One,
Get home by GCA."

The die was cast,
The moment past
To weasel out somehow,
The job at hand,
Take off and land,
Was all that mattered now.
We finished up
And had a cup
Of coffee dark and bitter.
What the hell,
A tale to tell,
When I'm a front-porch sitter.

We made a stop
At the PE shop
And suited up to fly.
Harness and vest,
G-suits, the rest;
Jocks dressed to do or die.
Then off with a roar,
Brave men at war,
To the duty desk, of course.
For you can't fly
Without clearance by
The paper part of the force.

Some wise wing wag
Gave us the tag
Of Noah Flight for chucks.
And that call sign
Was mighty fine
For us all-weather ducks.
Outside the door
A great downpour;
The base was like a lake.
The time was nigh
For us to fly
And bake a piece of cake.

I had a date
With three zero eight,
Parked out on the lonely ramp.
An F-4C
My ark would be,
To shield the wind and damp.
Soaked to the skin,
I got right in;
My GIB did the preflight part.
Canopy down
So I wouldn't drown,
I readied for engine start.

I hoped in my heart,
While waiting for start,
I'd stay a lousy spare.
It would be ideal
Not to turn a wheel,
Then bitch at the bar, "Not fair."
Well, that's OK,
But not today,
I heard a small voice say.
I had that feeling
I'd be dealing
With Lion and GCA.

We cranked as planned;
On the second hand,
J-79s did whine.
Post-start checks done,
I listened for one
To shout out the flight call sign.
When lead checked in,
Two followed him;
Three acknowledged in order.
But where was four?
Come up, you whore;
You best not ground abort 'er.

As though 'twere timed,
My crew chief chimed,
"I offer my regrets, sir.
Four's in the chocks;
Two busted clocks,
The pilot just Red Xed 'er."
"Rog. Thank you, Sarge,"
My voice boomed large;
I felt my rectum pucker.
The barrel game;
Guess who's the dame?
Spread 'em and grease up, sucker.

Got on the air,
Told lead that spare
Was ready to earn his pay.
Things ready now,
The problem how
To find the active runway.
Lead's voice came sour,
"Taxi tower;
Time that we be going."
After a razz,
They said with a dazz,
"Rog, Noah Flight. Start rowing."

Once more the gaff,
I had to laugh.
We, the best whores in the house.
Our only boast
Was screwed the most,
Weather, a douche and douse.
I looked for my chums,
Jerked my thumbs,
Then eased the power a tad.
Taxi light searching,
We went a-lurching
Out to the arming pad.

The wind did blow,
The viz so low,
I needed a taxi SID.
Taxiing blind,
I lagged behind,
And guess it's lucky I did.
Cuz two broadsided
And three collided;
Crunch went a wing tip and tail.
So scratch two and three;
They get home free.
We'll carry the GP mail.

Though quite alarming,
Soon we were arming,
Lined up abreast of lead.
With wind-forced grins,
They pulled our pins,
Quick checked with practiced speed.
The rains came down,
No runway crown,
The field awash in water.
How could we fly?
There was no sky.
I really thought we'd bought 'er.

My flying machine
Turned up green;
Ground crews scurried away.
It was time to fly
And probably die;
I turned to lead in dismay.
Then came a voice,
Dear hearts, rejoice,
I thought that God was speaking.
"Hey, Noah Two,
We're all through;
Hydraulic fluid leaking."

I couldn't believe
We had a reprieve,
An actual honorable out.
I played it cool,
Cuz that's the rule,
But wanted to sing and shout.
"Rog, understand;
The mission's canned.
Sympathetic abort here.
Let's shut 'em down,
Go downtown
For Lotus specials and beer."

"Rog, Two, sounds swinging.
Better than winging
Out on a rolling thunder.
I'll buy the Mateus."
Lead loose as a goose,
"Affirm, we're out from under."
Then 8th OPS called;
My heartbeat stalled.
The wing DO did spout,
"A super-bad show
If you guys don't go.
Maint'nance is on the way out."

Lead protested,
And he was bested;
Boy, he was bent out of shape.
Horns in his hair,
A chief got there,
With bailing wire and tape.
Strictly by the book,
He had a look,
Then came the fateful word:
"It's an overfill,
Just normal spill.
You've got an OK bird."

Leader mumbled,
My backbone crumbled;
Martin Baker held me straight.
Lead called number one,
You're clear, have fun.
We taxied to meet our fate.
Final checks made,
Last hopes did fade;
The colonel called and said, "Luck."
Thank you, big brother,
You ogre mother.
Light a Link Trainer and suck.

You jocks listen well,
Hear me, as I tell
The story of our going.
Lined up in the rain,
I can't explain,
How hard that storm was blowing.
Suffice to say,
Nature's display
Erased the lights and white line.
Spring loaded to leap
Through the runway deep,
Lead gave me the run-up sign.

I guess the chaplain
Must have been wrasslin'
Or passing the snakes around.
Or maybe wing
Gave heaven a ring,
'Bout getting us off the ground.
I tell you my prayers
Were added to theirs,
All hunkered down and brain-dead.
Oh please, somehow,
Move the leaking cow
Letting go from overhead.

Lead gave her the crop,
"See you on top."
His burners arced in the dark.
Then came the gift:
The weather did lift.
I saw the thousand-foot mark.
Well, it wasn't much,
Still no easy touch,
As if the pitcher lobbed it.
Holding the brakes,
I still had the shakes,
But counted ten and cobbed it.

We rolled fishtailing.
My GIB was bailing,
The nozzles coming open.
The runway river
Made me shiver,
But I kept on a-hopin'.
Speed-check abeam,
All gauges green,
The stick full aft in my lap.
Roll on, you whore,
A few seconds more.
Takeoff will be a snap.

The nose was lifting,
But we were drifting,
The edge of the runway near.
To drop a tire
Meant cartwheel and fire.
Come on, you big humpty, steer.
Just for a fraction,
We got some traction;
It bought us some precious time.
With saving grace,
We leapt into space,
Below us the mud and slime.

So off we went,
As though hell-bent,
My eyes glued on the gauges.
Tied on in trail,
A three-mile tail,
Skirting the storm's outrages.
The DME turned
As on we churned,
Outbound to be a hero.
Lead gave a shout
While climbing out:
"On top at two three zero."

My nose broke through
Into the blue;
I hurried to lead's wing.
Joining on the right,
I tucked her tight,
A puppet on lead's string.
We ginned along,
Over paddy and klong;
He yawed me on out to route.
"See ya, Lion.
Time we be tryin'
To give ole Invert a toot."

"Hey pervert, Noah,
Outbound Balboa,
Nearing the fence and squawking."
"It's Invert, Noah,
Charlie Balboa,
And man, the birds are walking.
But 7th says press,
Your chance of success
A snowball's chance, no doubt.
Best stay on this freq
So we can speak,
In case they cancel you out."

"Affirm, old buddy,
The clag's like putty;
Primary's probably clobbered.
Better by far,
To be at the bar,
Singing and getting slobbered.
But since we're up, gang,
We'll give her a whang,
Maybe luck into a hole."
"Rog, Noah. If not,
We'll give a sky spot,
Or alternate Barrel Roll."

We droned on over,
VFR clover,
Below us the murk and gloom.
Yeah, we did speed out,
Till TACAN readout
Fixed us over the pass of doom.
Orbiting stolid,
The stuff looked solid,
No reason to go down there.
Today's not my day;
I hear lead say,
"Hey, Two, I've got a wild hair."

He waggled a bit
For a tight two ship,
And said we were going down.
Despite my dread,
I nodded my head;
My whole world was turning brown.
Well, there were no buts,
Though lead was nuts
To leave the sky of clear blue.
Extending our boards,
We two vengeful lords,
Dropped into the glue like goo.

Hanging on one light,
I nestled tight,
"How 'bout your beacon, leader?"
And Holy Macro,
"Knock off the acro,"
I blurted as I keyed 'er.
Man, what a poling,
Barrel rolling;
I thought for sure we'd ding.
Vertigo devil,
My wings were level.
Calm down, shut up, and fly wing.

We drilled around,
Not seeing the ground;
Ten grand cooled lead's case of hots.
And that's close enough,
Cuz mountains are tough
When kissed at four hundred knots.
I hung like a champ,
On that one dim lamp;
Lead started us back upstairs.
When we topped out,
I wanted to shout,
So much for misplaced wild hairs.

Invert said, "High Hurt,"
Code words for divert.
Negative sky spot option.
So we racked up,
Toward our backup,
Heeding our ground-bound coxswain.
Laos was calling,
We went high balling;
Invert said contact Red FAC.
Real fighter jock sport,
Close air support,
Ranks next to a hirsute snack.

So we went grinning;
The war we're winning,
Or so all the papers say.
Our war machine
The best the world's seen;
A shame we can't have our way.
You say something's wrong,
We've been here too long,
Why won't they bend to our will?
Maybe forgotten,
Words to put stock in,
The name of the game is kill.

Now, I'm just a jock,
So I can't knock
Our leaders, statesmen, and such.
My job is flying,
Maybe farm buying,
For beliefs that mean so much.
But all the dissent
Over money spent,
The lives lost, some say a waste.
While both left and right
Continue to fight,
Holding their nose in distaste.

I'll tell you straight,
That war I hate,
Cuz I'm the guy that fights 'em.
But once we're in,
Let's go for a win.
Heavy the hand that smites 'em.
If game and candle
Be worth the gamble,
Then go for the throat and kill.
A war half fought,
Will be for nought,
And mortally wound our will.

So once elected,
War, the objective;
Wrap it up neat and fast.
It won't be pretty,
And that's a pity,
But better first than last.
Moral, immoral,
A senseless quarrel;
Winners are right in history.
I tell you once more,
The fact is in war,
No substitute for victory.

Yeah, I'm just a jock,
So I can't mock
The way the business is run.
My job's to fly,
Not reason why
The war's not over and done.
So pardon my tongue;
Impatient and young,
I tend to ramble a lot.
Maybe they're hurtin',
But one thing for certain:
It's the only war we've got.

There's no denying
It's great flying,
Regs loosened or revoked.
Pac One or Six,
Man, it's all kicks;
Assuming you ain't smoked.
When friends bust ass,
You raise a glass.
Behind self-erected wall
You're hard and you're cold;
A thousand years old,
You've been there and seen it all.

Once more ride with me
Approaching Sec C,
Somewhere south of Sam Neua.
The clouds broken here,
We called for a steer;
Red FAC came back all screwy.
Garbled and broken,
He drawled, soft-spoken,
We let on down to five grand.
"Reading you two by."
As we flew by,
He waggled and waved his hand.

Comm got better,
A max no-sweater;
Orbiting, we waited for smoke.
Red said with delight
An R & R site
Would bear the brunt of our yoke.
Well, that's mighty fine,
A target prime;
The folks back home are cheering.
His little prop job
Started to lob
Rockets into a clearing.

Smoke started rising,
Not too surprising;
Red urged we make a low pass.
"Look over the joint;
Spec your aim point
'Bout thirty feet left in the grass."
"Rajer, Red FAC-er.
We'll look, then whack 'er,"
Starting our low-angle run.
Would make your blood freeze,
We're in on the trees;
Now, this is my kind of fun.

So in we bombed;
My eyes, they glommed
On old sawhorses and planks.
Below a slight knoll,
A small water hole,
Tall weeds growing round its banks.
We called up Red.
He said, "Kill it dead."
Rog, no more inquiring.
Mils in, switches set,
High angle, you bet,
Six green GPs we're squiring.

I pulled to a perch,
Rolled in with a lurch,
And started to walk my pipper.
Going down the slide,
On lead's outside,
Cuz midairs really rip 'er.
I hit pickle height;
Airspeed was right,
Dive angle on the money.
A dollar a pound,
I rained 'em down;
So far the pass was bunny.

Sure of a bull,
I started my pull,
Keeping four gs on the bird.
The ground started winking;
I started jinking.
Below, a hornet's nest stirred.
Red buzzed in low,
Going quite slow,
Assessing our destruction.
We orbited high
In flak-free sky,
Awaiting his instruction.

Red's low slow pass
Near cost him his ass;
He took a couple of hits.
He really beat feet
Escaping the heat,
Plumb scared right out of his wits.
"Enough for today,"
We heard him say,
Heading for L-36.
We tagged along,
Case something went wrong,
And he went down in the sticks.

We flew a racetrack,
Going down and back,
His Bird Dog flying pretty.
36 in sight,
Everything alright,
Red started getting witty.
"I say, old chaps,
I've got the straps;
I can glide her home from here.
So thanks a lot
For getting me shot,
Also the cover and cheer."

"Our pleasure, Dad.
Glad you weren't had,
Breaking off to home plate."
Wanting last word,
Red sorta slurred,
"And Noah, your bombing great.
Not sure the amount;
I'd guess body count
'Bout forty fish KBA.
What's even more,
I'll credit you for
One picnic bench KIA."

Wasn't that nice?
Lead clicked the mic twice;
So much for a job well done.
With pegged VVI,
We climbed to blue sky,
Homebound to fifty-one.
Once more rushing through,
Impressive royal blue;
Lead was sucking his thumb.
Fuel check, a fast glance,
Near filled by pants,
Fuel quantity left me numb.

JP-4 poor,
Our little detour,
Had cost us a gang of gas.
Really up a tree,
Bingo minus three;
The crack became a crevasse.
I was hopin'
Udorn was open.
"Hello, Brigham. Say weather."
Brigham came back
With a story black;
Us with no props to feather.

"Brigham, we hanker
After a tanker.
It's the only chance we've got.
We'll keep steppin'
You check your weapon.
Interrogate every dot."
Max cruising posthaste,
So as not to waste
One drop of our precious fuel,
We waited right tense,
Nearing the fence,
For Brigham to check its tool.

"Noah, no joy.
Sorry, old boy."
Some days you can't make a buck.
Now what to do?
The great golden screw;
I guess we'd run out of luck.
I'm not blowing smoke,
We'd had the stroke;
All Udorn's Navaids inop.
To sum up our sad plight:
No fuel, no flight.
We'd step out somewhere on top.

All Thailand bases
Wore weather faces,
Ubon reporting the best.
We tightened our straps,
Stowed clipboards and maps,
As on to the south we pressed.
We'll fly to flameout,
There'll be a blame out;
Hope wing doesn't get too sore.
A nylon letdown
Will be our get down;
Sorry 'bout that, but it's war.

Yes, Phantoms would crump,
I'd make a jump;
Better to punch out than die.
Thus it was written,
But are you smitten
With pangs of remorse as I?
Well, some taxpayer
Offered a prayer
For me and my jalopy.
Tax-conscious fellow,
Turning yellow,
F-4s three mil per copy.

To Invert by now,
They'd found somehow
A wandering 135.
Our needed tanker,
South of brown anchor,
SAC out on a Sunday drive.
Soon came the vectors,
Our ground directors,
Invert and Waterboy too.
A kerosene feast
Was ours in the east,
After a rendezvous.

Skosh, we went liner,
About zero niner,
Our tanker running V max.
GCI talking,
Scopes we're hawking,
No time for us to relax.
After a hookup,
Things would look up,
We'd drink our fill, then decide.
Weather a heller,
The Clark ratskeller
Was just a two-hour ride.

Now gather round, gents,
My story's events
Are meant for the likes of you.
Keep nursing your beer,
As I bend your ear;
This tale is far from through.
My GIB and I
Continued to fly,
Painting our target ahead.
Exceeding low state,
We rushed to beat fate,
Low-level light glowing red.

Our spirits rallied
As cons we tallied,
Marking white on regal blue.
Those multi boobs
Coming down the tubes
Locked up, Vc gap at two.
Target confirmed,
Noses cold affirmed,
Thirsting for jet petrol ale.
We took a Judy,
Turned that beauty;
On rollout, we're one mile in trail.

Lead hurried to plug;
He took a fast slug,
Then disconnected for me.
Running on vapor,
Deft did I place her,
Hooked up and got some JP.
Then we played switch.
Lead started to bitch;
He needed more fuel himself.
No longer famished,
Flameout thoughts vanished;
I waited out on the shelf.

The boomer was good;
Lead hung like he should,
And told him we'd take a full shot.
The tanker came back,
"All we can hack,
Six thou, like it or not.
The destination
For this gas station,
Kadena; we're cutting it thin.
Besides the legs,
There's always the regs.
Our fuel is damn close to min."

So lead took gas,
Though voice bold as brass,
That tanker wouldn't yield.
So much for Clark;
The only ballpark
We'd play in was Ubon Field.
Lead disconnected
And then elected
To press on back to home drone.
Get spacing, save fuel,
A pretty good rule,
In case you're missed approach prone.

Lead waved good-bye.
My GIB itched to fly,
And slid us into the slot.
No belly-light glow;
He hooked like a pro,
And started to take our shot.
What a waste, I mused,
As we sat there fused,
Refueling going OK.
Two pilots, no need,
But jocks, they don't heed,
Appropriating away.

Yes, morale is low,
Retention's a blow,
And study groups keep weighing.
Hell, everyone knows
The answer, ROs,
Not more high-level braying.
Authorization,
Justification,
Deems the present crew manning.
So written in red,
Men, dollars, both dead;
Here's to shortsighted planning.

Excuse my high horse,
Again, I discourse,
But think it has bearing.
GIBs get a raw deal;
I know, hence can feel,
The hair shirt that they're wearing.
Still, with their fingering,
Let's not be lingering,
But press on with the story.
Recovery to go,
I want you to know,
Things still aren't hunky-dory.

We took our six thou,
Gave a porpoise bow,
Dropped off right. "See you round, Gramps,"
Replied the boomer
With timeworn humor.
"Rog. Forgot your green stamps."
Everything wired,
Pigeons acquired,
I spurred my camouflaged roach.
We flew for a while,
Out a hundred mile;
I called up Ubon approach.

"We're inbound, Lion.
It fit for flying
Round Ubon Air Patch this hour?"
"Noah, squawk flash,"
They said with a dash,
"Contact, info from tower.
Landing zero five,
Altimeter jive,
Weather, a hundred and one.
That's subject to change
To minimum range,
Before your approach is done.

"There's moderate rain,
Gusting winds, it's plain,
Yours, an unsavory stew.
Storm cells left and right,
Suggest expedite.
RAPCON to final for you.
Let's hope you sneak in,
Before it hits min,"
They added with derision.
"And if weather smarts,
Well, that's tough darts.
You'll get a good precision."

Now a hundred and one
Isn't much fun,
But shouldn't be a problem.
If the viz would hold,
The ceiling not fold,
We'd lick that bad-luck goblin.
Descent checklist,
No items missed,
Cockpit uncomfortably warm.
I lowered my nose,
Dropped into the throes,
Of a monster thunderstorm.

My gauges unwound,
We vectored around;
Turbulence bounced us a bit.
St. Elmo stopped by;
His fire did fly
Static electrical wit.
Descending, things oke
Until I smelled smoke;
You might say that I clanked.
Ram and dump max fast,
Decompression blast,
Smoke gone, lucky stars I thanked.

My lightning-like act,
Made my GIB react,
"Man, what the hell's the matter?"
"It's OK; wait one,
Till I'm done
With my radio chatter.
Lion, be advised,"
My voice stylized,
That of the old unshook pro,
"Emergency here;
Nothing to fear."
I'm speaking measured and slow.

I add sorta gruff,
"Just minor stuff.
Everything once again fit."
State my trouble?
I break the bubble,
"Cock fumes in my smokepit."
"Hey, that smoke you smell,
Is just a Pall Mall."
Thrown for a loss by my GIB.
"Disregard" mumbled,
The image crumbled,
No more professionally glib.

Just a small mistake
Anyone could make;
Wheezling won't get me far.
A boo-boo, then blooper,
A screwup super,
Deserved all hoots at the bar.
But now out of mind,
Cuz still in a bind,
The task: get down in one piece.
After safe landing,
Fun and glad-handing;
Right now, we're still in deep grease.

Passing ten or so,
I wanted to know
If leader made it OK.
When Lion advised,
I realized
That things better break our way.
He'd landed long,
Drag chute worked wrong,
Brakes locked and hair turnin' grey.
He started weaving,
Like greased owl leaving
The runway surface that day.

He slid and he skid;
Oh, the things he did
Would make a body wonder.
For extra spice,
He 360'd twice,
Amidst the rain and thunder.
Hook down, last resort;
I tell you, sport,
The odds against trapping great.
But long-shot players,
Long-answered prayers,
Came in when he took the tape.

"Rog, sounds thrilling,"
Downright bone-chilling.
I felt my stomach sicken.
For now 'twas my turn,
Maybe crash and burn;
The clag it seemed to thicken.
And who could foretell,
What kind of hell
Lurked in the murk below?
Though evil and black,
No use turning back;
There's nowhere else to go.

We descended to two;
GCA came through
To direct us as we groped.
We'd long overshot,
Therefore could not
Go straight in as we had hoped.
The storm rolled and crashed;
Onward we thrashed,
Around great rage and fury.
We were on trial,
Of that no denial,
Weather the incensed jury.

On a long base leg,
I started to beg
For mercy, such my concern.
Turbulence threw us;
The dolts, they flew us
Into their darkest return.
Violently knocked
Though harness locked,
G meter going berserk.
Then sudden, spat forth,
And still headed north;
Call it a lucky quirk.

With zero delay,
I told GCA,
"You best keep on your toesies.
Cuz if you make
Another mistake,
Man, I'll be pushing posies."
They rogered smart,
And said to start
My turn to final heading.
I drove standard rate
Through skies of dark slate,
Calm, despite inner dreading.

Straight and level now;
You guys know how
It goes inbound on final.
I rechecked weather,
With fate, slapped leather,
And got a verbal spinal.
To say it terse,
The weather was worse,
Not ameliorating.
Negative ceiling,
Viz was by feeling
And deteriorating.

Cut to the quick,
I clung to my stick,
Hand trembling on the throttle.
If I got down,
I vowed I'd drown
My body in a bottle.
Though overwrought,
That hopeful thought
Made it a more pleasant sky.
But first things first:
Before that great thirst,
Couple loose ends to tie.

Now, the rules are clear:
Maintain a veneer
Professionally unconcerned;
Take it all in stride.
Cross-check steely-eyed,
Remember the lessons learned.
Your IP's hounding,
The glare shield pounding,
You've been tempered hard and true.
So with a sneer,
Cast out fear,
Knowing full well what to do.

Controller verbose,
I listened, max close,
Each word chock-full of advice.
Everything dragging,
We kept on shagging,
Corrections small and precise.
"It's up to you guys;
I've gas for three tries."
Sweat running into my socks.
"Noah, fly your best.
We'll do the rest,
And talk you into the chocks."

Now, landing blind
Is not my kind
Of flying, sorry to say.
Though lots of glory,
More often gory;
I don't draw enough flight pay.
But I want down bad,
So I'll shave a tad,
And play on the razor's edge.
Good run, I assess,
Below mins I'll press;
On that, my solemn pledge.

The gate came and went;
I flew with intent,
Approaching the crucial stage.
Till fear and surprise
Locked my roving eyes;
I watched my gyro uncage.
Now, a lesser sort
Would have been caught short;
At first I thought ejection.
As moments ran by,
I switched to standby
And hoped for an erection.

Back on the line
And working fine,
I continued my approach.
Attuning my ear
To words loud and clear,
That came from my scope-bound coach.
Forward we sputtered;
I stick and ruddered,
To glide path interception.
Then descended, sir,
At six hundred per,
Toward uncertain reception.

The donut holding,
GCA scolding,
I listened and flew perforce.
Smooth my corrections,
Till their directions
On course, on glide path, on course.
Weather contrary,
Yet I didn't vary
One red, much sought-after hair.
Approach going well,
I reassessed, hell,
May's well come home with a flair.

An aberration,
Mental fixation,
Call it whatever you will.
I-want-downitis,
Malignant virus,
Often the kind that can kill.
Don't argue with me,
I'm no FNG;
I know the deck is stacked.
Don't bother to chide,
My drawing inside;
I tell you, we've got it hacked.

My reasons given,
Thus, I was driven,
Lashed by mental whip snappings.
Three hundred feet high
In a shroudlike sky,
Trying to shrug grim wrappings.
Then two hundred foot,
And black as soot,
No running rabbits around.
At a hundred feet
This is really neat;
No tally, no joy, no ground.

Double figures reached,
GCA preached,
"You're lined up; keep her comin'."
Passing seven five,
Downward I drive;
Controller keeps agummin'.
Now fifty to go,
And I don't know,
If this is so shit hot.
Almost there,
And I don't know where
Or what in the hell we've got.

Negative ceiling,
My gear was feeling
For concrete in that dark hole.
A wing and a prayer,
My radar soothsayer,
To him I consigned my soul.
About out of sky,
Touchdown was nigh,
And then, a hideous shriek.
The stick was slammed,
The throttle jammed,
Up the proverbial creek.

I was paralyzed,
Could not analyze
The fact that we were flying.
"I've got it," he yelled.
My GIB rocklike held
The stick; no use me trying.
Jeans I was creaming,
GCA screaming,
A panicky go-around.
Upward we soared,
Coal already poured,
Away from death and dread ground.

Homesick angel us,
I started to cuss,
Lucid once more; my words rung.
My GIB replied
With a diatribe,
Mostly in mule-skinner tongue.
Ranting and raving
About close shaving,
He claimed we'd been lined up left.
He saw flare pot light
Off to the right,
Reacted swift and deft.

"Ubon," I asked,
My anger masked,
"Confirm the runway lights out."
"Neg, Noah. We've light.
Flare pots on full bright.
Bit harder to see, no doubt."
"Thanks for informing,"
I felt like storming
But ended up with a sigh.
Cuz they're down there,
We're up you know where;
We'll give it another try.

Outbound we ginned,
On a long downwind;
At ten we started to bend.
"Noah, we're plottin'
A large cell squattin'
Off zero five approach end.
We greatly fear
Our MTI gear
Will not be up to the task."
State my intention?
Total dissension,
A hell of a thing to ask.

"Now look, GCA,
A cinch I can't stay
Up here just driving around.
My fuel's getting low;
Read through that snow.
Get me back down on the ground."
My order in,
With a stuck-out chin,
Chip on my shoulder swaying,
I flew to the groove,
To provide or disprove,
Fail and try again saying.

Honeycomb will,
Great effort, and skill,
I summoned for this approach.
If the gods would deign,
They'd ease the rain,
For us about to encroach.
But that hopeful thought
Would be for nought,
My tale of woe and worry.
No use prolonging,
Hammer and tonging
Things to hell in a hurry.

We were on glide slope
When GCA's scope
Went blank, a fuse or something.
Now towel to throw,
I got on the go,
Ass neatly wrapped in a sling.
I drilled about;
They gave a shout:
"We've negative precision."
You know what I said;
Don't know if they read.
"Me and horse I rode in on."

So things were max crit.
We jawed it a bit;
I asked for their suggestion.
Surveillance the key,
On runway two-three,
Was offered for digestion.
From trailer padded,
GCA added,
With a schizophrenic laugh,
"As we eyeball it,
We would call it
'Bout a hundred and a half."

Such was their claim,
In fact, wind and rain
Seemed less on the go-around.
So clutching at a straw,
On into the maw,
Heart switching to auto pound.
Lights of the city
Sparkled through pretty,
Orientating me well.
So downward I fly,
Shouting Ubon cry:
"Foxtrot, Sierra, Hotel."

Pinned on this flyer,
My hopes entire
I lined up with fuel for one pass.
Holding fast to zoom,
For punch-out room;
Onward, they're big and they're brass.
On course sticking,
Altitude ticking,
Lower and lower we got.
Would we get in?
The chances were thin;
I would not wager one baht.

Holding one eighty,
I goose my lady,
Ham fist in silk leather glove.
Sweet nothings mumbling,
Pre-climax fumbling,
I bring her down from above.
Told over the chains,
Every fiber strains,
As under some awesome weight.
In that dark valley,
Without a tally,
Breathlessly holding my mate.

Excited, hell yes.
More scared, I confess,
My blinker blinking a blur.
I spot the ground,
No runway around,
All sphincters and elbows, sir.
Then off to the right,
I spy dull light,
Twin rows little by little.
I yank and bank,
That beauty I plank,
Plunk her down in the middle.

We midfield slammed,
And almost crammed
The main gear up through the well.
Drag chute and brakes,
Hook down, for God sakes,
Fast as a bat out of hell.
Anti-skid quits
We've had the schnitz;
Braking turning sour.
Swerving and veering,
My nose gear steering
Useless, I call on power.

No good. My left tire
Drops into the mire;
I luck her back to concrete.
More aquaplaning,
Broadsiding, straining,
To keep that whore on her feet.
I try every ruse
And still she slews;
Don't know if I can cut her.
Approaching the tape
In parallel shape,
Frantically kicking rudder.

With seconds to spare,
I straightened that bear,
And felt the BAK-12 beneath.
The hook caressed
But didn't arrest;
I almost swallowed my teeth.
In ghastly straights,
Dealt aces and eights,
The queen of spades my kicker.
With no chance to draw,
I tell you I saw
And heard grim reaper snicker.

To idle cut off,
My coffin shut off,
Doing one ten I reckoned.
The end was near,
No overrun here;
Boonies' bone finger beckoned.
I thought of others,
Long landing brothers,
And all the small pieces found.
I started groaning;
My GIB was moaning,
A low and desolate sound.

First came a slight thump,
Then a bone-jarring bump;
Into rice paddies we flailed.
I felt the gear shear;
So great was my fear,
My personal nozzle failed.
Off on our belly,
Bouncing like jelly,
The radome dozing a road.
We were upending,
Metal was rending;
I thought for sure we'd explode.

At this point I knew
We wouldn't get through;
Expecting death's hand to knock.
Almost slow motion,
Such was my notion:
Sayonara, fair young jock.
Tip tanks and TERS,
Pylons and MERS;
The tail end starting to swing.
Over dike and ditch,
The son of a bitch
Swapped ends and wiped off a wing.

Screwed, blued, and tattooed,
More toolies we chewed,
Awaiting the fiery roar.
The slab had splattered,
The backbone shattered,
An engine left by side door.
In nought but a shell,
Still going like hell,
An apparition swooped down.
Mother, hands wringing,
Mournfully singing,
"Don't take your guns to town."

I blinked, she was gone;
Then Charon pushed pawn,
To finish the game perhaps.
My head was cracked,
I instantly blacked;
Slumping, I hung in the straps.
More pieces scattered,
Not that it mattered,
For I'll be changing address.
Bells of hell clanging,
Me, lifeless, hanging,
Off on the big PCS.

'Bout a half-mile drive,
Short of zero five,
Repose the battered remains.
A red pool of gore
On the cockpit floor
As hydraulic fluid drains.
Ah, peace, ah, silence,
No violence,
No more rivers to be crossed.
The good race run,
My journey is done,
Chips counted and cashed: I've lost.

Dead, I lay dreaming,
Till I heard screaming,
Calling me back from the grave.
Insane chuckling,
Hands unbuckling,
My GIB was there bold and brave.
"Get out," he's yelling.
"No foretelling,
How long this thing'll stay dud."
Senses regained,
I quickly deplaned,
Swan diving into the mud.

We left the crash scene
With our tails between.
Hard hoofing it, buns we moved.
Bowlegged leading,
GIB also needing,
New flight suit, telling signs proved.
Escape distance made,
Last respects we paid;
I recall my farewell cry.
"Burn now, you bastard.
Let's go get plastered,
Get some real mud in our eye."

Now troops harken more;
I still have the floor.
In truth, my tale about through.
I've taken your time,
With this lengthy rhyme,
The morals both far and few.
But I've heard some chucks,
Seen a few sage clucks;
I don't think it's been a waste.
And one point still nags,
So take last drags,
As I finish up posthaste.

Aftermath normal,
Reports logged formal,
Soon holding forth at the bar.
The booze and the talk,
I best take a walk,
Before it goes IFR.
I bail out alone,
A hooch-bound drone,
Fresh air clearing the way.
Ambling, reflecting,
My thoughts collecting;
I sure was lucky today.

From short stairs I bade
My small thanks in trade,
All the tomorrows to come.
Then scanned mistress sky,
Where men live, men die,
Sounding out war's dread drum.
I stood there pondering,
Mentally wandering,
Over flying, family, and fray.
Well, time to turn in.
I smile a wry grin;
Tomorrow's another day.

I opened the door,
And spied on the floor
A many-legged creature,
A thousand or two.
This bug I knew
Had a peculiar feature.
It could keep going,
Extra legs growing,
Regardless the numbers lost.
But I killed it dead,
Crushing its head,
When under my heel it crossed.

A fitting swan song
For this story long;
It's time to put her on ice.
This the last refrain.
I shan't abstain
From offering some advice.
It's a rule of thumb,
High and mighty some,
Apply grounded or in flight.
When you pull the stops,
"Keep your Mach up, Pops.
Happy Landings and Good Night."

Epilogue

Poetry has the greatest impact when read aloud. The language comes alive. Tone and texture add context and meaning. Listeners fashion images.

Reading aloud, you can be a Laurence Olivier and go for the full dramatic moment. Alternately, be a conversational Steve McQueen, slouching in an old chair or against the wall with a beer. Your interpretation is intensely personal. You want the moment to bring vitality to you and to others.

Vital to this book is a contemporary poem of the same name that challenges all of us.

Taps on the Walls

We build tall walls of different kind
For prisoners
Of war or crime or mind
Who serve or crouch and cry behind.

And if your freedoms you despoil
You prisoners
Cannot escape the toil
To stand and fight with mental foil.

Forced solitude, when doubts grow rife
Makes prisoners
Who build walls, struggling strife
Then tap the walls to regain life.

Afterword

The green cup featured on the back jacket was my only constant companion during six and a half years of imprisonment in North Vietnam. It was, like me, battered, scarred, and ill-used. Upon my release in February 1973, I smuggled it out.

During the Vietnam War, bracelets engraved with the names of POWs and MIAs were worn by caring Americans to show support for those captured or missing and for our families. When I came home, thousands of bracelets were returned to me and Myrna with messages from the heart. We answered all with a piece of ours.

On permanent display in Rockford's historic Memorial Hall, the cup and bracelets represent a great gratitude. My cup runneth over.

A final perspective: You really never leave combat. It is a lifetime thing. The glory and the gore continue, enlarged or diminished by time. If you have been there, you know.

Nations and people wage war and endure the perils and costs because of perceived interests, fear, and hate. As Eric Hoffer wrote, "Man is the only animal willing to fight and die for an idea." If we have learned nothing else, it's that violence should be carried out quickly and decisively. It saves lives and money on both sides and preserves public support. Robust airpower provides the nation with that option.

We engaged gradually in Vietnam and, predictably, blood and treasure were squandered. In 1973, we disengaged under the Paris Peace Accords, and in 1975, the North conquered the South and reunified the country. We lost the war.

In 2002, Myrna and I went to Vietnam with a White House Fellows delegation. As we traveled from Saigon to Hanoi, one fact stood out: We won the war too. Vietnam and its people have high regard for Americans and are much attracted to our way of life.

The delegation met with Võ Nguyên Giáp, the former Commander and Defense Minister of North Vietnamese Forces. When I was introduced to him, I greeted him in French. *"Je vous connais bien, Générale Giáp."* ("I know you well.") He replied in kind and took my hand, and together we walked into his conference room, where a scheduled ten-minute meeting lasted an hour. The questions were polite but direct. There was a strange warmth between us, perhaps a sense of affectionate sadness. You never really leave combat, but you feel differently about "the enemy."

It's time to leave this book. Because the messages are many, I hope you revisit often. Many too are the blessings of a lifetime. Truly, the cup doth run over.

Glossary

7th: 7th Air Force in Saigon; the Air Command in Vietnam.

8th: 8th Tactical Fighter Wing, nicknamed "Wolf Pack."

135: C-135 tanker aircraft for in flight refueling. Always a lovely sight to behold.

AB: Afterburner; a pilot engages the jet engine afterburner for maximum power and acceleration.

Adana: Location of an air base in Turkey used by the USAF and the Turkish air force.

AFB: Air Force Base.

anvil top: Cloud formation of a large thunderstorm.

APM: All pilots meeting.

BAK-12: Cable barrier, an emergency stopping system using a tailhook that catches an arresting cable. It works well most of the time.

Balboa: Mission code word for the day.

Barrel Roll: Mission to northern Laos.

beacon: Radio-signal-based navigational aid (nav aid) for pilots and navigators.

B-52 Stratofortress: Large, multiengine long-range bomber in active service from the 1950s to the present.

bingo: Radio code word for reaching minimum amount of fuel needed to return to base (RTB). As in a radio call "Viking is bingo," meaning I have minimum fuel remaining and need to go home—RTB.

Bitt: Bitburg; site of a U.S. air base in Germany.

black D on white square: Aircraft marking signifying the 100th Bomb Group, known as the Bloody 100th or the Hard Luck Group due to high combat losses.

blinker: Cockpit indicator that shows flow of oxygen.

blivet: A large metal tank, travel pod, or practice bomb attached to the aircraft.

BLD: Boulder City, Nevada, TACAN (tactical air navigation) near Lake Mead.

boards: Speed brakes, used to increase drag/slow down or descend.

boonies: Boondocks; the middle of nowhere.

B-24 Liberator: WW II bomber.

break: The pilot's pitchout maneuver over the runway prior to landing. Also a maximum hard turn to escape enemy fire, as in "Viking, break right"—normally called by a wingman.

Brigham: An air-control and radar site in Thailand.

Bunker Beacon: A WW II navigational radio beacon used to rendezvous aircraft for bombing missions.

button G: The guard channel is a radio frequency "normally" reserved for emergency communications.

cack: Bad trouble.

CAVU: An acronym for "ceiling and visibility unlimited" —good, clear flying weather.

CBs: Big, building cumulonimbus clouds that often involve poor weather conditions such as thunderstorms.

center: Shorthand for "air traffic control center," which monitors and regulates flights.

Charlie: Another radio communications term for Roger or Rog, meaning "understood." Also a nickname for the Vietcong (VC)—the enemy.

Charon: The boatman on the river Styx in Greek mythology.

Christmas tree: The lights on an aircraft warning-light panel. When they come on during a flight, it usually means serious trouble.

clag: Clouds, rain, and turbulence—not good "stuff" to fly into.

Clark: Air Force Base in the Phillipines.

clank: Mentally overloaded, as in "clanked up."

clearance: Authority requested from and given by center.

close air support: Dropping ordnance in support of ground troops or on targets identified by forward air controllers.

CNX: Cancel.

contrails: Condensation trails.

C sub L max: Term for when an aircraft has insufficient lift to keep flying normally and enters a stall condition.

Cuban 8: Acrobatic maneuver that forms a horizontal figure 8 in the sky.

CU: Pronounced "cue." Embedded CU means turbulence or hidden thunderstorm.

CV: Aircraft carrier.

Cyclone: Engine on the B-17, Flying Fortress.

Dash 1: Flight manual.

DO: Director of Operations.

DR: Dead reckoning—using map, speed, and time to navigate.

DRV: Democratic Republic of Vietnam. North Vietnam.

external tanks: Fuel tanks hung on aircraft wings or belly.

FAC: Forward Air Controller: Pilots assigned ground and air duties to identify targets to the fighters.

farm buying: To die, as in "buy the farm." A retirement thought hardly ever achieved.

fence: term used for crossing into hostile territory—time to arm up.

F-4C: The Air Force version of the McDonnell Douglas F-4 Phantom; a long-range, twin-engine two-seat fighter.

field-grader moon: Field-grade rank is major to colonel. A full moon makes it easier for the "old guys" to fly and thereby compensate for less lift in the night air.

fifty-one: TACAN channel for Ubon Air Base. Ubon is a city in eastern Thailand.

final: The last mile or so before landing.

flight level (FL): Altitude term for height above 17,099 feet—i.e., FL 180 equals 18,000 feet.

FNG: F'ing new guy.

form 5: Official record of flying hours and qualifications.

Fort: The Flying Fortress—the B-17, a four-engine heavy bomber with a ten-member crew.

Foxtrot, Sierra, Hotel: F Bomb, Shit, Hate—a fairly crude but common Ubon Air Base curse with a lovely roll of the tongue mellifluence. Contrasted with Sierra, Hotel (Shit Hot), which means great.

frag: Fragmentary order detailing air combat tasking for the day. A piece of the overall air battle plan for the day or longer.

full stop: A landing that ends in taxiing to parking versus making a touch-and-go.

g: Force of gravity. 2 gs equals twice body weight. It takes 4 gs to do a loop. Fighter pilots must deal with 7 to 9 gs.

gate: Navigation aid or point close to runway to assist landing in bad weather.

GCA: Ground-controlled approach/precision-radar approach, where the air-traffic controller uses radar imaging to instruct the pilot to a point where a safe landing can be made.

George: Air Force base near Victorville, California.

GIB: The "guy in back." The aircrew member in the rear seat of a two-seat fighter like the F-4.

GPs: General-purpose bombs—normally the 500-pound variety.

Green Sixteen: Inexperienced flyer usually stuck on the outside of the flight formation.

g-suit: Corsetlike garment for the stomach and legs that offsets force of g by filling with air.

Guernsey run: A milk run or easy flight.

Gulf of Tonkin: Gulf along the coast of Vietnam, off the South China Sea. The Gulf of Tonkin Resolution gave President Lyndon Johnson the right to use military force without getting a resolution of war from Congress.

Hahn: Air base in Germany with the worst weather in Europe.

"hog": The F-84, a turbojet-powered fighter-bomber that began as a straight-winged aircraft and evolved into a more traditional-looking swept-wing fighter jet. Also the A-10 Warthog.

hook: Tailhook to catch the cable or barrier on aircraft carriers, and for emergency land-based landings.

hundred and a half: 100-foot ceiling (altitude of the cloud cover), half-mile visibility—not bad, but not good either.

IFR: Instrument flight rules, created by the Federal Aviation Administration for flying using only aircraft instruments because visibility is so poor.

in hack: In big trouble.

Invert: An air-control and radar site in Thailand.

IP: Instructor pilot.

ITO: Instrument takeoff, normally in trail formation (planes taking off 10 seconds apart).

J-8: An attitude indicator in older aircraft that shows the position of the aircraft relative to level flight (when it worked—it had a bad habit of precessing, or locking up).

jocks: Fighter jockeys (pilots).

JP-4: Jet fuel (also JP-8).

J-79: GE jet engine (there are two in the F-4).

Judy: "Taking a Judy" means taking away control of the intercept from the ground controller.

Kadena: U.S. Air Force base on Okinawa used by tankers.

KIA/KBA: Killed in action/killed by air.

Kirtland: U.S. Air Force Base in Albuquerque, New Mexico.

letdown plate: Paper depiction of arrival procedures for an airfield.

liner: Maximum range airspeed.

Link Trainer: A flight simulator . . . emphasis "simulator."

Lion: An air-control and radar site serving Ubon Air Base in Thailand.

Lotus Specials: Restaurant in downtown Ubon famous for its "tizzling platters."

L-36: A secret base in Laos.

Mach: Speed relating to Mach 1 speed of sound—Mach up is good.

marking: Leaving contrails in the sky.

Martin Baker: Manufacturer of the F-4 ejection seat.

Mateus: A Portuguese rosé wine, a favorite back then; not now.

McGuire: Air Force base in New Jersey, named after WW II flying ace Major Thomas B. McGuire, Jr.

Mils: A unit of measure used in adjusting the bomb sight.

Minuteman: An ICBM, a long-range missile with a nuclear warhead.

MTI gear: Moving target indicator instruments that provide aircraft ID in bad weather.

Mu Gia Pass: A mountain pass that was the principal entry point between North Vietnam and Laos on the Ho Chi Minh Trail.

Nellis: Air Force base north of Las Vegas, Nevada, known as the home of the fighter pilot.

NORDO: No radio; unable to transmit or receive.

Norton: Air Force base in California known for its all-night weather briefing.

NOTAM: Notice to airmen; new flight and airfield information.

nozzles: Exhaust nozzles opening, indicating a good afterburner light.

OD: Officer of the Deck; in charge of the ship when the captain is absent.

OPS or ops: Operations Officer; squadron second-in-command or command center.

Package One: Southern North Vietnam.

panels: Runway markers for distance to runway's end.

PCS: Permanent change of station, or to a new base. "Big PCS" means "to die."

PE shop: Personal equipment—helmet, g suit, harness, guns, etc.

Phantom II: The F-4 fighter.

piece of cake: Easy to do, often a statement of bravado.

pigeons: Directions.

pilot's halo: Framed outline of the aircraft on an undercast when the sun hits at a certain angle.

Pipper: Predicted impact point, bomb site indicator.

PIREP: Pilot's weather report.

positive control: Airspace about FL 180 in the United States controlled by center; must be on instrument clearance.

precision radar: Very good ground capability to help with landing approach—provides directions and glide slope.

radar: Used to track in-flight activity and provide a precision approach to landing.

radome: Radar dome on the nose of the aircraft.

Ramstein: U.S. air base in Germany.

R & R: Rest and recuperation.

RAPCON: Radar vectors to approach.

RAYDOE: Laredo AFB, Texas.

Red X: Not fit to fly; maintenance code.

Rolling Thunder: Code name for missions in North Vietnam.

RON: Remain overnight.

ROs: Radar Operators or weapon systems officers.

Route One: Vietnam's main highway, which runs north to south from the Chinese border to the Mekong Delta.

RTB: Return to base.

running rabbits: Approach lights that flash and point to the runway.

schnitz: Like cack–bad trouble, violent death a possibility.

Sec C: A heavily defended area in Northern Laos.

short snorter: Dollar bill signed by buddies and always carried during WW II and the Korean War. Failure to do so meant buying a shot—or snort—of booze for friends.

SID: Standard instrument departure; the flying directions on instrument departure.

sky spot: Dropping bombs at the command of ground radar sites, very inaccurate.

Son Tay raid: A brave American commando raid on a prison camp near Hanoi to liberate POWs in November 1970. The camp was empty and the result was that most POWs were relocated to Hoa Lo prison (the Hanoi Hilton). This was the first time that POWs were put into large group cells of forty or more and communications were established throughout the camp. A big mistake by the captors.

sortie: A single flight or a specific mission.

Spang: Spangdahlem Air Base in Germany.

Split S: An aerial maneuver that reverses direction of flight by rolling to your back and pulling to the vertical and then pulling out before you hit the ground. It works if your plane is high enough.

squawk flash: To hit a switch that electronically lights up your aircraft on radar.

Starlifter: C-141 cargo aircraft.

surveillance approach: Direction only, no glide-path information.

swung: Passing over or by a navigational aid.

tap code: Method of forbidden communication for POWs.

TAC Attack: Tactical air command magazine (fighter-pilot oriented).

TACAN: A navigational aid providing direction and distance to or from a point.

TERS and MERS: Racks for holding bombs.

tool: Slang for "radar."

T-33: A two-seat training and utility aircraft from the 1950s and 1960s.

trooping the line: Formal review of troops. In this case, going up and down the flight line.

Tuba City: A town and navigational aid east of the Grand Canyon on an airway.

Ubon: Fighter base in eastern Thailand.

Vc gap: On-board radar indication of aircraft closing velocity on target.

VFR: Visual flight rules; generally means good weather.

V max: Maximum capable aircraft speed.

VVI: Vertical velocity indicator; indicates how fast you're going up or down.

Waterboy: Another air-control and radar site.

WOXOF: Pronounced "walks off"—means zero ceiling, zero visibility, obscuration fog (not good).

Yalu: Yalu River separating North Korea from China.

Zero eight or Zero four: Runway designation by direction—recalling 360 degrees in a circle. For example, 08 is a runway headed 080, or almost east (090); being east as 180 is south, 270 west, etc.

General Borling's major decorations as pictured opposite the opening of Section IV: Defense Distinguished Service Medal (2), Air Force Distinguished Service Medal, Silver Star, Defense Superior Service Medal, Legion of Merit (2), Distinguished Flying Cross (2), Bronze Star with V (Valor) Device (2), Purple Heart (2), Meritorious Service Medal (2), Air Medal (6), Air Force Commendation Medal (3), Prisoner of War Medal, Combat Readiness Medal, Air Force Good Conduct Medal, National Defense Service Medal (2), Vietnam Service Medal (4), RVN Gallantry Cross with Palm, Republic of Vietnam Campaign Medal.

Acknowledgments

Credit and thanks are due to Colonel (IL) J. N. Pritzker, IL ARNG (Ret.), Founder and Chair of the Pritzker Military Library, and his Chicago team at Master Wings Publishing, notably Mary Parthe and Lisa Lanz. Their support and drive to succeed made *Taps on the Walls* possible and then a reality.

Thanks also to Scott Manning and his team in New York. Harriet Bell, the erudite editor; Charles Rue Woods, for a masterful design and layout; Roni Axelrod, for driving the print train with RR Donnelley; and Betsy Hulsebosch, for marketing and social media initiatives. Scott, as the quarterback and publicist for this effort, merits a standing ovation accompanied by shaking heads as to why anyone would be in this business.

I am very grateful to Senator McCain for his words in the foreword. He represents a special courage and respect and really cares about our country. I saw all that up close.

Finally, the buyers of this book deserve plaudits for their desire to read (aloud, hopefully) the prose and verse in *Taps on the Walls* and understand the reality and utility of creation and walls.

About the Author

JOHN BORLING, MAJOR GENERAL, USAF, Ret., chairs the business board and is a director of Synthonics, a specialty pharmaceutical company advancing a patented chemistry that markedly improves performance of selected existing and pipeline drugs. He is also a director of Ascent Exploration, a Texas oil and gas company, and an advisor to ADKOS, a vehicle storage company.

He founded and chairs SOS America (Service Over Self)—www.sosamerica.org—a patriotic organization advocating military service for America's young men aged eighteen to twenty-six. Previously, as president and CEO of Chicago's United Way, he was credited with a rebound of interest and annual campaign success exceeding $95 million. In 2004 and 2006, maintaining that America needs a political middle, he ran for a seat in the U.S. Congress but was unsuccessful—obviously a better fighter pilot than a politician. A motivational, political philosophy, and business speaker, he is in demand across the nation.

A native Chicagoan and Air Force Academy graduate, his military career spanned thirty-seven years. A highly decorated officer, he was an F-15 Eagle fighter pilot and commander of the famed "Hat in the Ring" squadron. He commanded an Air Division at Minot AFB, North Dakota, and directed Operations for Strategic Air Command (SAC). In that position, he directed SAC's support of hostilities in the first Gulf War and Panama and was charged with execution responsibilities for the nation's nuclear war plan. At the Pentagon, he led CHECKMATE, a highly classified war-fighting think tank, and was Director of Air Force Operational Requirements, helping initiate a new family of guided weapons. In Germany, he commanded the largest fighter and support base outside the United States and later served at NATO's Supreme Headquarters in Belgium, working directly for the Supreme Commander and Chief of Staff. He was central to the creation of HQ North in Norway and served as Chief of Staff of that integrated NATO/National Command. He has piloted many aircraft, including the F-16 Viper, the F-4 Phantom, the SR71 Blackbird, the U-2, and B-52 and B-1 bombers. During the Vietnam War, he was shot down by ground fire. Seriously injured and captured while trying to evade, he spent six and a half years as a POW in Hanoi.

Borling is a graduate of the National War College and of executive programs at Harvard's John F. Kennedy School of Government and Harvard Business School. He was a White House Fellow and, later, treasurer and director of the governing foundation and for many years a regional selection panel member.

Current civic activities include: Life Member of the Commercial Club of Chicago, Trustee of the Lincoln Academy of Illinois, President of the Sister Lakes Michigan Land Conservancy, Inductee, Illinois Aviation Hall of Fame, Who's Who in America, plus numerous other local and national organizations.

John is married to his high-school sweetheart, Myrna. They live on the Rock River in Rockford, Illinois.

John & Myrna,
Graduation Day, Pilot Training
Laredo Air Force Base, 1964

John & Myrna,
At Home, Rockford, Illinois,
2012